Black Diamond

A Stark Springs Academy Novel

Book 1

By Ali Dean

Chapter 1

"I so do not belong here." Taking a deep breath, I admit to my friends listening eagerly on the other line, "I'm pretty sure this scholarship was a huge mistake. Someone in the admissions office at Stark was smoking crack, you guys."

It's not just the humongous mountains, bigger than any I've seen in New England, or the fancy buildings and cars I noticed as the airport shuttle drove through Stark Springs, Colorado. It's a gut feeling that I don't belong here. I've had it once before, at my first Nor-Ams race in Maine six months ago. Nor-Ams races are the level just before the World Cup races, and I'd barely qualified for the one in Maine.

"Girl, relax," my best friend Chelsea Radner tells me, her voice sounding a little distant on speaker. "The shuttle dropped you off, what? Twenty minutes ago? Give it at least another twenty minutes before you make any rash decisions."

"Come on, Chels, we all know Roxie deserves this scholarship. She's going to rock those stuck-up Stark bitches and they won't know what hit them." Tyler Luck, Chelsea's boyfriend, is convinced I'm the next Lindsey Vonn or Mikaela Shiffrin even though I've only had one noteworthy top-ten finish, and that was most likely a fluke.

"The girls there already giving you a hard time, Roxie?" Brad's concern makes me straighten my spine. He was the only one who seemed less than thrilled about this opportunity. Brad Samuel has been my friend since the first day of kindergarten, and I can't blame him for worrying about me here, without anyone to have my back. Still, I don't want to fuel the fire.

"No, I've only met a few girls in my dorm. They're a little snobby but nothing I can't handle. It just seems like these kids were destined at birth for a life in competitive winter sports, if their names are any indication. Listen to this -- the three girls I've met so far are named Aspen, Winter, and Telluride."

Chelsea's laughter fills the phone.

"Telluride?" Tyler asks dubiously.

"She goes by Telly."

"Aspen and Winter aren't that crazy," Chelsea offers when she's recovered. "They're sort of cool, actually. What are their sports?"

"Aspen's a snowboarder, Winter's a figure skater, and I didn't catch Telly's sport."

"Your roommate has a normal name," Brad points out. "Monica Danvers, right?"

"Yeah, she's not here yet." We'd Googled Monica as soon as I found out she'd be my roommate. All I know is that she's a figure skater from Michigan.

"You're there to train," Chelsea reminds me. "This is just a chance to train with the best for one, maybe two years, and get free travel to competitions at the next level. If you decide after one year that it's not for you, just come back to Ashfield for senior year."

The door to my dorm room opens and a tiny black-haired girl walks in carrying a giant duffel bag. A woman who must be her mother, if the sleek black ponytail and petite frame mean anything, rolls a suitcase behind her.

"Hey guys, looks like my roommate's here. I'll call you later."

After hanging up, I introduce myself. "Hi, I'm Roxie Slade."

"Monica Danvers, and this is my mom, Donna." Even Monica's voice sounds delicate. She's got an authentic, friendly smile though, and that tells me a lot. The girls who greeted me at the dorm gave me those fake smiles that say, "I'm pretending to be nice in case you end up mattering to my social standing, but mostly I'm just judging you and deciding whether to hate you outwardly or behind your back."

"When did you get in, Roxie?" Donna asks me.

"Oh, just a few minutes ago."

Donna glances around the room. "Is this all you have? Do you need any help moving stuff in?"

I glance at the two large bags by my twin bed. "That's it. I dropped my ski bag off downstairs. That's where this girl named Telly told me to put it."

"Telluride Valentini?" Monica's voice sounds funny when she says it. "You talked to her?"

"Yeah – she said she was the dorm rep? She was out front when I got here. I think she's in charge of making sure the new kids find their rooms."

"Yeah," Monica says with a nod. "That's right. She's the student representative for the dorm so she's in charge of move-in day, things like that. She's always scared me a little." With that admission, I decide I like Monica. You actually have to be kind of brave to admit fear, especially when it's fear of a peer. Telluride looked like she could bench press Monica with one arm.

"What's her sport?" I ask. If she was an alpine ski racer, I'd know. I might not compete with the best, but I know who they are, and which ones go to Stark Springs Academy.

"Hockey," Donna answers for me. "She's one of the girls who grew up in Stark."

"So, why Telluride then? Isn't that, like, a rival ski town?"

"Her parents met in Telluride. It's sort of romantic, I guess," Monica says, but she's rolling her eyes.

I grin at her. "Anyone here named Stark?"

Donna and Monica share a surprised glance. "Uh, no," Monica says with a dismissive shake of her head.

I wonder if their surprise is at the idea that a parent would give their child such an unfortunate name, or if there's something else. I mean, Stark doesn't seem that crazy given the girls I've met so far.

Monica and her mom ask a few basic questions about me, but they seem to already know I'm a ski racer from Vermont.

"Are your parents here, Roxie? Did you all drive from Vermont or fly?"

"Just me. I flew into Denver and took the shuttle. It's crazy expensive to fly into Stark Springs."

Donna nods. "Monica and I like to make a little road trip out of it every year. We've been doing it since the eighth grade, right kiddo?"

"Mom, you've got to stop calling me that. I'll be seventeen soon."

"Anyway, we brought the pickup and packed it full, so if there's anything you need, I'm sure Monica's got it. The closest Target is 100 miles away, so if you didn't pack it, you'll have to order it on Amazon."

"Yeah, I've got a toaster, mini fridge, space heater, blow dryer, and like, seven thousand bottles of lotion because my skin wilts at this altitude. I'm well-stocked. You sort of lucked out being my roommate." Monica's voice remains delicate as she gains confidence around me, but it's becoming more sing-songy. I could listen to her talk all day.

"Awesome. Since all I've got is ski stuff and clothes, I'll help you unpack. What do you stock in the fridge, anyway? Isn't there a cafeteria?"

"Yeah, but I like having..." She stops mid-sentence as her eyes zero in on the doorway.

When I follow her gaze, I understand her inability to speak. A male model is standing in our dorm room. A rugged one, at that. And slightly familiar. It's not the broad shoulders and athletic build that make me unable to stop staring. Though I'll always give a nod of admiration to a fit dude, with friends like Tyler and Brad, muscles don't get me all worked up like some girls. It's the piercing turquoise eyes, a color I've only seen in photographs of the

Caribbean Sea. Light brown hair curls underneath a ball cap, but the boyish style doesn't diminish his dominating presence.

"Hello Monica, Mrs. Danvers." The smooth voice holds a note of intimidation that I don't like.

Feeling Monica shift beside me, I tear my gaze away to look at her. She's blinking at the doorway with a strange expression on her face. Is she afraid of this guy like she is of Telly? Or does she have a crush on him? Either way, she's speechless.

"Hello, Mr. Black. What can we do for you?" Donna asks. I'd almost forgotten she was still in the room.

"I'd like to introduce myself to our new student," he says.

"Hey, I'm Roxie Slade," I tell him, taking a step in his direction. I notice two other guys standing in the hallway, watching us.

But instead of staying to help with the introductions, Monica and Donna excuse themselves to get more things from the car, and the two guys in the hallway follow them down, leaving me alone with the male model. When he shuts the door behind them, I'm suddenly very uneasy. Though the Danverses mentioned having more things in the pickup, it seems like it was a coordinated effort to get me alone in a room with this dude.

"How was your trip from Vermont?" he asks, crossing his arms and staring right at me. Okay, so he already knows where I'm from. Noted.

"Not bad. There aren't a ton of flights out of Vermont so I had to leave crazy early, but no delays or anything so that's good." Why is he here and why is he asking about trivial things?

"You flew into Denver?" he asks, as though he already knows the answer.

"Yeah, cheaper," I respond with a shrug. "There's a shuttle that was pretty easy. How about you? Where are you from?" I'm pretty sure this must be Ryker Black, but I don't know where he's from. Even if

Donna hadn't said his last name, I've seen photos of the guy in magazines and on the internet. He's far more striking in person.

"I'm from Stark. Do you know who I am?" he asks quietly. What a cocky bastard.

"Mr. Black, of course," I imitate Donna's formal greeting. I don't want to feed his ego, but Donna did use his name, and well, given I'm at Stark Springs Academy, I'd be an idiot not to figure out who he was anyway.

"You can call me Ryker," he offers, as if it's a privilege to do so. "I'm here to help you get settled at Stark, and to help you learn the ropes about how things run around here." The explanation feels heavier than the words themselves. I just nod, still uncertain what he wants from me, if anything. Is he some sort of student rep like Telluride?

"Have you had any problems since you arrived?" he asks.

"No, why?"

"If you have any problems, come to me. I'm the one who handles problems at Stark."

My hands go to my hips. "I can handle my own problems, Black."

"I go by Ryker or Mr. Black," he says, ignoring my statement. "It's important that Stark continues to live up to its legacy, and there are rules here to ensure that happens. I hope that you will follow them."

"Dude, what is your problem? You're a student, not the headmaster." Is this some kind of joke?

"The headmaster follows my rules too."

Clearly, Ryker Black is deranged. Donna and Monica will be back any minute, so I'll just have to humor him for the moment. It's a pity the guy has some mental issues. He's such a rock star on a snowboard, I wouldn't have expected it.

"I've read the school handbook, Ryker," I say gently. It's a lie, mostly. I skimmed some of the policies, but the only rules I remember thinking would be annoying were dorm check-in by 8:00 PM on weekdays, and no opposite genders allowed in dorm rooms without the door open and all four feet on the ground. Chelsea and I laughed pretty hard at that one. Apparently no one cares about the door being open though.

Ryker takes a deliberate step forward until he's all up in my space. What a weirdo. "The first rule is that the handbook policies mean nothing. You'll learn the rest as you go. Monica can tell you about what happens if you don't follow them." And with that, he spins around and leaves.

What the hell just happened? I'm tempted to call Chelsea and fill her in on the weirdest conversation of my life, but I've already called her twice since I landed in Denver, and Monica and Donna will be back in a minute.

I'm about to unpack my bags but I can't help myself. I climb onto my bed and peek out the window overlooking the dorm entryway. He might be mentally unstable, but I'm intrigued. His two friends are standing outside the dorm while Monica and Donna haul the mini fridge out of the pickup. The guys don't offer to help. Ryker comes out a moment later, followed by Winter and Aspen.

With her white-blonde hair and pale skin, I almost laughed when Winter introduced herself. But apparently it's not a nickname, according to her Wikipedia page. She's the reigning junior national figure skating champion. Now, she's taking a step toward Ryker, and he's shaking his head as she reaches to touch his arm. She immediately drops her hand at something he says. And then he ignores her, turning to the guys with a nod. At that, the three of them walk over to the Danverses' truck and begin unloading. Ryker picks up the mini fridge and nearly runs over Winter and Aspen on his way back inside before they jump out of his way. The girls watch him with dropped jaws and I can't tell if they're just gawking at his hotness or find it surprising he's helping Monica and her mom. I'm guessing the former, since in my opinion, any decent guy would offer a hand. Right, so Ryker's decency remains questionable.

But this means he's coming back up, and I can't decide whether I want to experience another weird conversation. Though apparently he still has girls like Winter Lovett pining for his attention, despite his strangeness.

Ryker doesn't say another word to me, and neither does anyone else, as we unload the rest of the pickup. Aspen and Winter hold the front door open but otherwise simply stare us down as we pass back and forth. It's awkward as hell and I'm determined to get some answers from Monica as soon as we're alone.

"I'm going to let you settle in, kiddo, while I check in at the hotel," Donna tells Monica. "We'll get brunch tomorrow," Donna says before kissing Monica on the cheek and waving goodbye to me. "You're welcome to join us, Roxie."

"I have my first team meeting tomorrow morning, but thanks for the invite."

"So nice to meet you, Roxie."

As soon as the door closes behind her, I turn to Monica. "Okay, what is the deal with Ryker Black?"

"What did he say to you?" Monica asks.

"Some shit about following rules, and that the rules in the student handbook don't mean anything. The guy's a little not right in the head, huh?"

At that, Monica jumps up and takes my arm and then drags me out into the hallway. "You can't say stuff like that," she whispers. "He might be listening."

"Um, what?"

"He might have bugged our room, Roxie," she whispers, glancing nervously around the hallway.

"Why would he do that?" It sounds to me like Ryker Black could use some mental health counseling.

"Look, let's get ready to go over to dinner, and I'll fill you in on the way, when we're outside. Just don't talk about Ryker Black in our room." She spins back inside and unpacks toiletries and a towel. "Are you going to shower? There are three stalls on this floor and you can borrow any of my things." Monica's sing-song voice is back, and I'm totally confused.

"Yeah, I guess I'll get cleaned up." It's been a long day of travel and weirdness. Maybe a shower will help clear my head. I can't shake the feeling that I'm missing something major about Stark Springs Academy. I'm beginning to wonder if this place is more than just a boarding school for winter athletes. What have I gotten myself into?

Chapter 2

Monica keeps glancing at me as we make our way out of the dorm. "What's the problem, Monica?" I can tell she wants to say something.

"I'm just surprised by you."

"How so?"

"It's your first social thing at Stark, and you just pulled whatever out of your bag, threw your wet hair into a bun, and called it good. Most girls would have changed like, twenty times, and spent forever on hair and makeup."

"Really? The people I've seen so far seem pretty casual. You're not dressed up or anything."

"True. We're always between workouts, so students usually just wear comfortable stuff, but still, some girls spend a lot of time on the comfortable look, if you know what I mean."

"Yeah, I guess." I don't really know what she means, but I want to hear about why she thinks our room is bugged, so I drop it. "Tell me about Ryker Black. What's his deal?"

Monica looks around before speaking. "He runs this school, Roxie. And if you don't follow his rules, things won't go well for you."

I'm tempted to laugh, but hold it in. "Isn't he a junior, like us?"

"Yes. He's eighteen though. Most of the guys here were held back a year in school early on so that they have an athletic advantage. Except for the figure skaters."

"Seriously?" I guess that doesn't surprise me as much as her other revelation.

"Look, Ryker is fair. If you do what you're supposed to do, he won't bother you. Just train hard and don't step on his toes, and you'll be fine, okay?"

I glance over at Monica, now trying to decide if she's the crazy one. "Are you going to explain why you think he'd bug our room?"

She sighs. "It's unlikely, but I wouldn't risk it. You know why you're my roommate? The girl I was supposed to be roommates with got kicked out at the end of last year. Olga Popova. She'd been at Stark since the seventh grade. They found cocaine in her locker."

"Oh, shit. She was your good friend? Did you know she was into that stuff?" I'm surprised to hear it. Though there are plenty of kids at Sugarville High back in Vermont using drugs, it's not something I would expect of the athletes at Stark.

"She wasn't," Monica says meaningfully. "That's my point."

"You're saying someone made it up or planted the drugs?"

Monica purses her lips but doesn't answer. "Everyone knew Olga didn't do drugs. She's one of the best figure skaters in the world. But that was the whole point. She didn't go back to Russia because she has a cocaine problem, Roxie. She went back home because that's what Ryker wanted."

Monica is essentially spelling it out for me, but I'm not ready to accept it as truth. "Wait, I still don't get what this has to do with our room being bugged."

"Ryker might not trust me, because Olga was my closest friend here. And you're new, so he doesn't trust you, either. We almost never get new students as juniors. You're a potential threat."

"A threat?" I'm about to burst into laughter again. I've looked at the alpine ski roster and I'm definitely the least accomplished racer at Stark for my age. Even some of the freshmen racers have more experience than me. Is my lack of experience the threat?

"A threat to the way things run around here. But don't worry, you'll figure it out." Monica doesn't sound too confident.

When we finally get to the cafeteria, I haven't decided if Monica is the delusional one, or if it's Ryker. Something isn't right about what she's telling me, that's for sure.

I'm half-listening to Monica tell me about the various dining options as I take in the cafeteria, or DH, as Monica keeps calling it, short for "dining hall." It seems a more appropriate title anyway, since the place looks more like a restaurant than the cafeteria at Sugarville High School. There are trendy lanterns hanging above round wooden tables, and actual chefs wearing tall hats and white aprons stand behind three different food lines.

"Can we get whatever we want?" I ask Monica.

"Yeah, you just tell them and they serve it for you. Leave room for dessert though, there's a fro yo machine."

"Fro yo?"

"Frozen yogurt."

I fill my tray with chicken parm, pasta, and garlic bread. The salad bar looks pretty awesome too, but I'll have to save that for another time. Who cares about the crazies at Stark when there's food like this at every meal?

Monica waves to me from a table and I begin to make my way over there before I'm intercepted.

"Hello, Roxanne." Ryker stands in front of me, and even with a hoodie and baseball cap shading his eyes, the vivid color draws me in.

"Why do you call me that?"

"That's your name, isn't it?" he asks.

"No one calls me Roxanne. Unless you're my mother and you're pissed at me."

"I like it," he says with a shrug. "Come sit with me." He turns around like I'm going to follow him, and begins to walk to a table where the two guys who helped us move earlier are sitting. Telluride is there as well, all six feet of her.

It doesn't take me more than a second to decide. I'm not being rude. He's the one who didn't wait for my answer and I'm not going to ditch the first person who's been friendly to me.

But when I put my tray down next to Monica, she looks like she might have a heart attack. It's then I realize that all the attention in DH has shifted. To me.

"Roxie, what are you doing?" she whispers.

"Sitting with you. What's the problem?" I sit down and pick up my fork.

"Did you not hear anything I said on the way over here?"

"I'm not breaking any rules, am I?" I ask with a frown.

She closes her eyes and shakes her head like this is her worst nightmare. "Go sit with them, Roxie. Now."

Ignoring her, I take a bite of chicken. DH is almost silent. I glance around, taking in students as they stare unabashedly at me. I'd noticed some staring when I was getting food, which I took for being new, but now I know it's because Ryker Black spoke to me. People are whispering, probably passing along that I chose not to sit with him. Ridiculous.

"How's the salmon?" I ask Monica.

"Roxie, you're making your life a lot harder by defying him," she says quietly. "I've got friends joining me, okay? You don't have to sit here because you feel sorry for me, if that's it. Believe me, you're making my life harder by sitting here, too."

That just pisses me off. "You don't want me here?"

"No! I mean, I would, but not now that..." She drifts off, tilting her head in the direction where Ryker is sitting. She can't even look over there.

"Monica, I thought you were cool a few minutes ago. I thought we were going to be friends. But if you're going to let some deluded control freak dictate who can sit with you when you eat, then I'm out."

I don't look back to see if she's relieved, angry, or hurt by my words, but I do glare at everyone else staring at us, including Ryker, when I make my way over to an empty table to eat my dinner.

Maybe I should be worried that cocaine will be planted on me and I'll be the next Olga Popova, but I just can't bring myself to care at the moment. I mean really, how in the world is it possible for a kid one year older than me to have that kind of power? He might be devastating to look at, but it's not like his eyes are capable of hypnotizing people. Or maybe they are. Maybe I'm really at a wizard school, and I don't know it. Smiling to myself at that thought, I glance over to Ryker's table. He's typing away on his iPhone, apparently having already forgotten about me.

I finish eating quickly, not in the mood to linger, and fill a cone with fro yo to eat on my way back across campus. But when I get to the dorm building, my key card won't let me in. I briefly wonder if Ryker has the capability to alter student access cards, but brush it off. Monica's just paranoid, and it's rubbing off on me.

I decide to kill some time while waiting on someone going into the dorm building. Sitting down on the front step, I pull out my cell phone. I've got to call my parents and tell them things are going well. But I hate lying to them. They both get on the line and fire so many questions off, it's easy to avoid the truth. How's the weather? Your dorm? What's your roommate like? Is Stark Springs as beautiful as it is in the pictures? Did your luggage make it? How was the flight?

As their only child, I know they're feeling my absence. They both keep busy working at the Ashfield general store they've owned for twenty years, but I know I'll need to give them regular updates to keep them sane. My parents actually pushed the hardest for me to take this scholarship. They know I've missed opportunities to compete at important races, and they blame themselves. But I've had everything I've ever needed. It's not like we're poor. Ski racing is just an expensive sport.

I'm contemplating whether or not to call Chelsea when I see a figure walking in my direction. My fists clench as I take in the hoodie and baseball cap. If he's not mentally ill, he's the world's biggest asshole, as far as I'm concerned.

He doesn't take his eyes off of me as he gets closer, and my pulse begins to quicken in preparation for... something. A battle, I suppose.

"What do you want?" I call out, determined to break his icy glare first.

He doesn't answer until he's standing right in front of me and I rise to my feet so I'm not looking up at him. Well, I'm still looking up, but not as far.

"You didn't listen to my warning earlier. I was only trying to help you out." It's not a friendly tone.

"I don't recall breaking any rules."

"You're smarter than that, Roxanne," he says with a tilt of his head. "The only unwavering rule is that I'm holding your future in the palm of my hand. If you aren't in my good graces, you won't be eating, you won't be training, and you certainly won't be going to the competitions."

I suck in a breath, and prepare a comeback. But he cuts me off.

"We've all been here for longer than you have and the rest of the students respect the way things run around here. If you continue to challenge me, you won't last at Stark." His voice is strangely gentle, almost pitying, and I resist the urge to smack him.

He leans forward then, reaches around me so it almost seems like he's coming in for an embrace, but just when his nose is inches from mine, I hear the door beep open behind me.

"Your card will be reactivated tomorrow. Remember that. Because if you leave tonight, you're sleeping outside."

I remain speechless as he turns and leaves. There's nothing I can do but walk up the stairs, where I'll be a prisoner in my dorm for the rest of the evening.

Chapter 3

Monica never came home last night. She either spent the night with someone else, or Ryker decided to deactivate her card as well, and she spent the night outside. My best guess is that she's avoiding me, either because Ryker told her to, or because she's afraid that associating with me will get her expelled.

After a fitful night of sleep, I'm still not sure whether to play along and bow down to the all-mighty Ryker Black, or fight it and risk getting the boot. Really though, I'm still finding it hard to accept that Ryker Black holds my fate in the palm of his hand. It's easier to believe he's just your everyday sociopath and has a few gullible students fooled.

As I make my way across the quad, surrounded by brick and stone buildings and filled with clear mountain air, my body hums in anticipation of meeting my new teammates and coaches. The buzzing in my chest overtakes my worries about Ryker Black and his rules as I remember that I'm about to meet two ski legends, Rocco Moretti and his younger sister, Lia Moretti. They've both won Olympic medals in every discipline – slalom, giant slalom (GS), super giant slalom (super-G), *and* downhill. I mean, no one's in their league. No one in the world. In history. And they will be coaching me.

Neither competes anymore, and instead of settling down in their home country of Italy when they retired from racing, they decided on Stark Springs, Colorado. Rocco came about a decade ago, and Lia maybe five years later.

And then there are the people who will be on my team. Just thinking about all of it has me sweating with nervousness. But it's a good feeling, almost like standing at the starting gate, looking down at the course.

"Roxie Slade from Vermont!" a cheerful voice with a European accent calls from behind me. I turn cautiously, having learned where the students' loyalties lie at Stark.

"Hi?" I glance at the girl, about my age, and try to place her. She's definitely familiar.

"I'm Ingrid Koller. We were both at the Nor-Ams downhill last February in Maine. I had goggles and a helmet on though, so you probably don't recognize me." Ingrid smiles broadly and it softens her sharp features. She's got a good two or three inches on me, and I'm already taller than average. She also probably outweighs me by at least thirty pounds of muscle, and I'm not exactly weak.

"You Stark people gave off a 'don't talk to me' vibe, so I don't think I actually spoke with any of you," I admit.

She laughs. "Yeah, we're not supposed to talk to the competition, or even like, ride on the lift with them. We all knew you had applied though. We were secretly spying on you," she says conspiratorially. "And now you don't have to say *you Stark people*. You are one."

"Am I?" I'm not so sure about that. There's a lot of things wrong with what Ingrid just said, but I decide not to dwell on it as we open the doors and I walk into the most magnificent sports complex I've ever seen. It's all sleek modern lines, high ceilings, and giant windows. We're overlooking a giant atrium, and above us is an indoor track.

Ingrid takes in my awe-struck expression and tugs me forward. "Come on, you'll get the whole tour in a few minutes."

I try to keep my cool as Ingrid leads me down the stairs to the group of people milling about in the atrium. It's hard to pretend like people aren't staring at you, sizing you up, when, well, when they're doing it so blatantly. Surely some of them were at DH last night and know I've already committed the unforgiveable sin of not sitting next to Ryker as he requested. I want to smack some sense into these people, but instead I try to pretend I don't give a damn. I mean, I don't. Or I wouldn't, if I didn't have to.

"Welcome to Stark, Roxie." With the Italian accent, I know who it is before looking over at my new coach. "Rocco Moretti, head alpine coach. Call me Rocco." He reaches out to shake my hand and I can't help my star-struck response, which is silence.

I nod mutely. It's the best I can do.

When Rocco asks me what I think of Stark Springs so far, I don't mention Ryker Black. "The mountains are big," I say lamely.

Rocco chuckles. "That they are. We'll be starting dryland training this afternoon, and you'll be well-acquainted with them before the first snow."

"When do you guys usually get out on skis for the first time?"

Rocco shrugs. "Depends. We have access before the resort officially opens, so as soon as there's enough packed down to set up a few gates, we'll be out there. Usually early November."

I'm excited to work hard, in whatever capacity. That's what I'm here for. But dryland training never gives me the rush that I get making turns on snow.

After a few minutes, Rocco has us stand around in a giant circle to introduce ourselves. It seems this is mostly for my benefit, except for the seventh graders. There are six of them, and, during introductions, it appears everyone on the team started at Stark in seventh, eighth, or ninth grade. There are about fifty of us total, ranging in age from twelve to nineteen, and nearly evenly split by gender. More than half are European, and I'm the only one from Vermont. That's not surprising, given how many ski academies are in my home state.

The last people to introduce themselves are the team captains, Petra Hoffman and Sven Teslow. Petra is more of what I expected, based on the things I've seen and heard about Stark skiers. She doesn't smile as she tells us what we already know, that she grew up in Germany, and moved to Stark Springs at age ten. She doesn't mention that her father is one of the Olympic team coaches or that her mother won several gold medals in the eighties, but her haughty posture tells us she expects us to know that already. Even though I can tell right away I won't like Petra, I admire her racing résumé.

Sven Teslow is all blond, classically handsome, and looks like he could lunge his way up Stark Mountain while holding me above his head. But he's not especially tall, about my height, maybe 5'8" or 5'9". For some reason, I'd imagined that everyone from Sweden was incredibly tall. Sven seems to fit the rest of the stereotype, with pale blue eyes that are currently staring right at me.

"I'll be giving the gymnasium tour to all the new members. Follow me," he commands with a nod before walking in my direction and then right past me. His arrogance reminds me of Ryker, but I follow him, since I do need the tour.

It's just me and the seventh graders, who keep glancing my way with curiosity. Is it really so unusual to be new as a junior at Stark? When Sven shows us a swimming pool, and I ask if there's a swim team, even the twelve-year-olds looks at me like I'm an idiot. The indoor pool has eight lanes and it's the nicest lap pool I've ever laid eyes on, so I think it's a fair question.

"It's for cross-training," Sven explains.

"Will we use it?" I ask.

"Probably not. It's not part of our program. The Nordic skiers use it sometimes, and occasionally the skaters or injured athletes. It's just here if we need it."

That becomes a theme as the tour continues. The tennis, racquetball, and basketball courts are all "here if we need them." No wonder they had plenty of money for my scholarship. I don't feel quite so guilty about it now.

The last stop is the weight-lifting room, and we can hear Eminem letting loose before Sven even opens the door.

"You'll become well-acquainted with the equipment in here over the next few weeks," Sven explains. "It'll back off once the snow comes and we can hit the slopes, but until then, you will be spending a lot of hours looking at these four walls."

At least the walls have mirrors, I note as I take it all in. It's the first room we've been in that's filled with people, and I hear one of the seventh graders say his name before I see him.

"That's Ryker Black," he whispers to the kid next to him.

My eyes follow where he's looking, and I find Ryker in the mirror, shirtless, and doing overhead squats. Whoa. What an image. It doesn't seem like it should be legal, this guy working out shirtless with others around to watch. There's something inherently naughty about it.

Before I can look away, his eyes find mine and hold me there until he finishes his set. There's a challenge between us, but something else too, and it has me feeling hot and sweaty, like I'm the one who just did the reps.

"Hey Sven, you gonna introduce me to the newbies?" another shirtless guy says, and I take in his tattoos and shoulder-length hair before noticing he's looking at me and flashing a smile. I recognize him as one of the guys who came by the dorm with Ryker yesterday. He's cute, that's for sure, but not as devastating as psychopath over there.

Sven doesn't answer right away, and I notice him glance at Ryker before replying, "No, Player, wasn't planning on it."

Player? Ouch. The guy must have a real reputation to get a nickname like that.

"Are you Player Westby?" one of the seventh-grade girls practically screeches. I think her name is Carla.

"That's me," tattoo guy confirms with a wink. Yeah, he winked at a seventh-grade girl. And he's got to be at least eighteen. Gross.

"Oh my gawd! My friend from home is going to freak! Can I take a selfie with you to send to her?"

"Sure," he says with a roll of his shoulders.

Carla squeals and pulls a phone out of her back pocket.

I'm feeling a little out of the loop. Maybe I need to do some more research on the students at this place. I've never even heard of this guy, and apparently he's famous.

"You want a selfie, too?" Player asks, stepping closer to me after taking the photo.

"I'm not going to lie, dude, but I don't know who you are. Should I?" I give him another once-over.

He grins widely. "Just a burnt-out snowboarding prodigy. And I think I already know who you are -- Ms. Slade, is it?"

"So, Player, huh? Is there a story behind that?" I'm not trying to flirt, but I can tell this is the kind of guy who takes everything that way, if he's in the mood.

He tosses his hair out of his face. "Nope, just what my mama named me."

"Really?" I ask dubiously.

"Player, go do squats," Ryker's voice interrupts us.

Player glances at Ryker, then Sven, who's shaking his head, before peeking at me for a moment. Without a word, he follows Ryker's orders.

I can't help myself, I cross my arms. "You are quite the tyrant, Mr. Black."

When he lifts his lips, I almost mistake it for a smile.

"Sven, I'll take over Roxanne's tour from here."

"This was the last stop, Ryker," I tell him, though I'm not entirely sure that's true. We're back near the atrium where we started, so it's a safe assumption.

I hear Carla murmuring about Ryker Black. "But, if you have the time, I'm sure my buddy here would love a selfie with you."

I glance at Carla, whose mouth is formed in an O, and leave before Ryker can say anything. What am I doing? I thought I'd decided to play by his rules? I just can't seem to submit to his ridiculous display of authority. And besides that, I get all... worked up when he's near me. I needed to get out of there.

The atrium is empty except for Ingrid when I come out of the weight room.

She frowns. "Where's Sven?"

"Finishing the tour. I bailed."

Ingrid's dark eyebrows rise in question.

"Don't ask. What are you doing here?"

"We finished the team meeting, thought I'd see if you wanted to grab something to eat with me before our first workout in a couple hours. Oh, and we'll need to get your locker and combo. That's what Sven does at the end of the tour."

"Oh," I say stupidly. I don't want to admit it, but maybe I'm overreacting where Ryker is concerned.

"No problem, I've got you covered." Ingrid takes my arm, and I let her lead me back in the direction I came. "Was the snowboarding team in here?" she asks as we approach the weight room.

I tense, and Ingrid notices. "What?"

"Yeah, they're in there. Why do we need to go to the weight room?"

"To get your locker combination. Ryker keeps the list. I thought I saw him going in there with Player earlier."

"Oh, shit," I breathe out. "I'm really going to have to start being nice to that guy, huh?"

Ingrid stops right in front of the door, and her easy-going demeanor shifts. "What did you do?"

"I just kind of, um, walked away when he said he was going to take over the rest of my tour. I mean, he singled me out, and he acts so high and mighty, and I just didn't want to deal. It's not like I was mean." I'm rambling, and Ingrid is shaking her head with pursed lips.

"You don't understand, Roxie," Ingrid says fiercely. "Ryker Black isn't acting that way because he's arrogant; he acts that way because of who he is."

She sees the confusion on my face, and I wonder if she realizes her words make no sense. At all.

"Ryker is royalty, okay?" she huffs out, like it's obvious. "Think of it like this, Prince William is to Wales as Ryker Black is to Stark Springs. Well no, it's bigger than that. He's like the ruler of winter Olympics and pretty much anything winter sport related. The companies who make your skis, ski boots, the chair lifts, he owns them."

I blink at her for at least a full minute before I can respond. "His family owns a lot of the business in the winter sport industry?" I ask, trying to sum up what she's telling me. "So we all have to bow down to him? That's stupid."

Ingrid shakes her head. "Maybe I didn't explain it right. It's more like mafia than royalty. And since his dad, well -- his dad isn't running things anymore. So Ryker Black is basically the mafia boss of winter."

Chapter 4

The mafia boss of winter? What is *wrong* with these people? I'm about to burst out in laughter, I can feel it rumbling in me, but I know that if I do, I won't be able to stop. And Ingrid looks so serious, almost *afraid*. It sobers me. She seems to really believe what she's saying.

Sure, I'd heard of Ryker Black before coming here, even though I don't follow snowboarding very closely. But his name buzzes around Sugarville Mountain, and I suppose I'd always thought it was simply his snowboarding accomplishments and good looks that gave him such notoriety. Really, he must be giving these Stark Springs kids some serious Kool-Aid. Either that, or this is some elaborate new-girl joke and we'll have a good laugh about it when they finally get to the punch line.

The door swings open, nearly smacking me in the forehead. Ryker's eyes sweep past Ingrid before landing on me. He looks like he might blow past us but reconsiders.

"Can I get you something?" he asks darkly. "Change your mind about the tour?" Why does everything that come out of his mouth sound like a threat?

Breathing in deeply through my nose, I force out the words, "I didn't know that the locker room was the last stop. Ingrid informed me that you give out the lockers and combos. Will I be getting one or did I lose my opportunity?"

Ingrid laughs nervously. "She's trying to apologize, she's just not very good at it."

I glare at her.

"That depends," he says, ignoring Ingrid, "on whether you are willing to do something in return."

I'm about to cross my arms, but refrain. Crossing my arms signifies fighting mode, and I need to remain calm, cool and collected. At least he's thrown a shirt on. That helps.

"We can discuss it on the way to the locker room. Ingrid, I'll make sure Roxanne makes it to the mountain at two for the workout."

Ingrid lifts her hand in a little wave, but her expression says she's worried about me. What does she think he's going to do? Stuff me in a locker?

Ryker takes my hand and begins walking down the hallway. It's such an odd and unexpected gesture, I don't react at first. But then I remember he's a jerk and I snatch my hand away. I do follow him though, as he walks briskly down two flights of stairs to the basement level, unaffected by my rejection of his hand. It seemed to be more of an effort to ensure I came with him than anything else.

He holds a key card up to a heavy door, looks around, and pulls me inside, letting the door shut behind us. We're in an office, not a locker room. And even though, after everything I was told, I should be terrified, I'm not. Just curious.

He stands inches in front of me, breathing hard, and then pushes me lightly so the backs of my knees hit the leather chair behind me, and I'm forced to sit and look up at him.

"I'm prepared to make a compromise, Roxanne, since you are clearly struggling with the way we do things around here. I won't take away all your privileges, if you can follow a few simple rules."

"What privileges?"

"Access to DH, your dorm, the weight room, the locker room. I could just take away your scholarship, Roxanne, but you haven't done anything egregious enough to warrant that. You will, though, if we don't set things straight." My scholarship? Does he really have that kind of authority or is he bluffing? I'm still convinced I'm being punked here.

"Where are we?" I ask, looking around.

He takes his index finger and pushes my chin back so I'm facing him. "My office. Don't change the subject." His *office*? He has his own office in the gymnasium basement?

"So aside from doing stupid things you ask like sit with you or go on a private tour, what other rules do you expect me to follow if I want to eat and sleep?"

"Don't talk to me like a bratty kid, first of all." For the first time, there's a light ring to his tone, borderline flirtatious, if I didn't know better.

And when he says it like that, I realize that's exactly what I'm doing. But he's acting like an unreasonable parent, so what does he expect?

"I'll work on it."

"Don't flirt with anyone."

I frown. Back to the harsh scary voice, I see.

"Don't date, kiss, or have any kind of romantic interaction with anyone."

"Does everyone have this rule?"

"No, but there are variations depending on the situation."

I'd push it, out of curiosity, but these rules don't really bother me. I'm not here to flirt or date or kiss or any of that anyway.

"I will not approach you on campus, but you will agree to meet with me once a week on my terms."

Standing up, I push him back. "That's ridiculous. Why would I do that?" I suppose the dating thing is ridiculous too, but maybe he wants everyone focused on their sports, which isn't so crazy. Dating can be very distracting. I can't imagine why he and I would need to meet though.

"You're the first student at Stark who's started after freshman year without some sort of connection to the Academy. You have no legacy, no relatives who've attended in the past, yet you've been given a scholarship. I need to keep tabs on you. I'll be contacting you with the location and time to meet. Oh, and one more thing. Try not to call me a deluded control freak in front of half the student body."

I narrow my eyes, uncertain if he means to threaten or tease me about what I said to Monica at DH. He doesn't sound angry about my words last night, which were pretty ugly, I'll admit, but he's not giving much away.

"And if I do these things, you won't make my life miserable?" I almost slip out something about planting cocaine, but I don't want to get Monica into trouble, just in case this isn't an elaborate joke.

"We may need to amend as things proceed, but that can be discussed at our weekly meetings, if necessary."

My eyes narrow at that. I can't do this, play by his stupid rules, without more of an explanation. The ones provided by Ingrid and Monica are just not cutting it for me.

Ryker is still towering over me, looking like he's ready to wrap up this business meeting. But I have to know.

"You seem to know everything. So, why am I even here? Why did I get this scholarship?"

"Why do you think?"

Sighing, I lean back in the leather chair. It's really pretty comfortable. Spins around in circles and everything. I give a little kick and twirl around a few times. It feels like anything I tell this guy, he'll already know, but I humor him for the moment.

"I'm from Vermont. There are five awesome ski academies within a two-hour drive from me, and one in my hometown. Problem is, none of them could offer me a full-tuition scholarship, or much of anything that would make a difference for us. I wasn't about to let my parents pay, like, half their annual income for me to go to an academy. They offered to try, but it wasn't worth it to me."

Ryker moves to the desk beside me and hops up. Without his hat on, I can see the sharp angles of his cheekbones, the curve of his jawline, the absurdity of his long eyelashes. His light brown hair is slightly curly, and a few locks tuck under his ears. It looks soft.

"You trained with the Sugarville Academy kids for free, but you weren't actually a student there." Ryker looks at me, and I'm not surprised he already knows these things. He's shown he makes a point of knowing everyone's business.

"Yeah, the teachers at my high school, the public one, were flexible with me skipping classes and stuff, but it wasn't ideal. I mean, the Academy kids pretty much have tutors to accommodate their training and racing schedules. Plus, even though I got free coaching and equipment, the travel costs to some of the big competitions were just too much. I stuck with the local races, and there are plenty of good races in New England." Well, that wasn't so true anymore. After placing eighth in the downhill at a Nor-Ams race, it was clear I was ready for the next level, which involved racing all over North America and Europe.

"How did you get into ski racing, anyway?" Ryker asks. He watches me intently, and I see genuine interest there. I'll admit, ski racing isn't usually the kind of thing people fall into, particularly if you have parents who don't ski at all, like mine.

"I grew up in Ashfield, right next to Sugarville Mountain, and my friends growing up would take me. Their parents are skiers, and they were happy to let me use their hand-me-downs and stuff. I was a scrawny kid, and I had to work hard to keep up. When my friends started ski team at age seven, I begged my parents to let me join too. I didn't know then how expensive it was. But they did it. After that first year, triple-S -- Sugarville Ski School -- gave me scholarships for the coaching and I had sponsors for equipment by age twelve."

Why am I telling this guy my life story? It's those damn turquoise eyes, so beautifully framed with dark lashes, that make me want to open up. They don't match his harsh personality. Am I telling him about me in hopes he'll soften a little, see me as a real person, and understand how huge it is for me to be here?

"Do your friends go to the Academy?" Ryker takes his bottom lip in his fingers and tugs, and I wonder what he's thinking. Is he getting this information from me to use against me? Why does he care? And as he rolls his lip between his fingers, I wonder what that gesture means. He seems almost nervous, but I can't imagine why.

"Yeah, my three best friends started in the eighth grade, like most students do at Sugarville Academy. The ski academies in Vermont aren't anything like Stark though." As I say it, I remember he knows all about the ski world already, but he tilts his head, encouraging me to continue. "For starters, they're hardcore about skiing only, at least at Sugarville. A couple academies in the area have snowboarding teams now, too, but usually they are separate, not part of the school. And even though the ski academies back home are expensive, they aren't, um, like super-fancy."

"Fancy?" he asks with an amused expression. He's looking more relaxed as I talk, and he's starting to seem like a real person now, so I keep going.

I roll my eyes. "They don't have chefs in white aprons and facilities like these," I say, pointing around in a circle in reference to the building I just toured. "It's more... basic." Realistic, is what I almost said.

Ryker nods thoughtfully, but doesn't say anything.

"You never answered my question about why I'm here," I remind him.

"You never answered mine about why you think you're here."

I glare at him. I suppose I did get a little off track. I'd forgotten about where I was going, with him looking at me like every word out of my mouth was crucial, and asking me questions that seemed irrelevant.

"I think I'm here because I hit top-ten at the downhill Nor-Ams race in Maine last season, and someone at the admissions office, or Rocco, or whoever makes these decisions, thinks I'm good enough to have a shot at making the team. The national team," I clarify, for his benefit. Amongst ski racers, the ultimate goal is to make the national team, and between each other, we just call it "the team." I wonder if that's the case here at Stark, as well, with many athletes trying to make the national teams for different countries. "Anyway, as far as the scholarship that includes every expense, including travel to competitions, I'd wondered about that, but now I see this place has plenty of money to throw around."

Ryker just stares at me for a moment, and then he smiles. If I thought the guy was devastating before, I'm in so much trouble now. His entire face lights up, and there's nothing I can do to stop the smile on my own face from mirroring his.

"You're here because *I* picked you, Roxanne," he says softly. His voice is warm and gentle, so even though his words are troubling, I don't react. "There are talented skiers all over the country, but we don't mail application materials to all of them, and we certainly don't accept every talented skier to the academy."

"Well then, why me?"

"I've watched you race before. You have what it takes. On the slopes, that is," he says lightly, and I wonder if he's teasing me. Is Ryker Black capable of something like teasing? It seems too juvenile for him.

I've been told before by random coaches and racers that my tenacity on the hill is exceptional to witness. It never meant as much to me as Ryker's words just now. And when did he watch me race, where?

"Some students have full scholarships, like you, but not many," Ryker continues. "It doesn't really matter to us whether you pay your tuition, but you'll find that many people here, particularly on the alpine team, come from Olympic blood, wealth, or both."

"Olympic blood?" I scoff. It's got that winter mafia ring to it again. "What about you, Ryker? Snowboarding hasn't even been an Olympic sport for very long, so it's not like your parents were snowboarding Olympians."

He raises his eyebrows, and I can't tell what that means. Am I supposed to know about *his* bloodlines? Olympic, mafia, or whatever they are.

"I used to ski race, Roxanne," he tells me, and I wait for him to elaborate, but he doesn't.

As we continue to watch each other, I have the strange feeling that he wants to cross this barrier between us, the one where he holds all the power. His shoulders are still stiff, his gaze cautious, but he wants to melt into the moment, forget his rules and his status. Or maybe it's just me, realizing my attraction to Ryker Black is very dangerous.

The air in the small office crackles. It's silent, but the tension is so strong, I'm certain Ryker feels the energy snapping in the space between us. The few times I've let anything happen with a guy, I'm the one who's made the first move. Yeah, some guys have tried to make a pass at me, but I'm not shy about saying no. I've always been fairly decisive when it comes to these things.

The first time I kissed a boy, I knew I didn't want him to be my boyfriend. He was a racer from Canada, in Sugarville for a competition, and I was determined to see what this kissing stuff was all about, since Chelsea had already done it with several boys -- before she and Tyler got together, of course. It was sloppy and not very appealing.

The second time was this past summer with the captain of the Sugarville High hockey team. I'd always thought he was cute. He'd asked me out a few times over the years, and I always turned him down. I didn't really want to date the guy, and I knew I'd be leaving for Stark in a few weeks, so I decided a summer fling was acceptable. Colton Lennox definitely had enough experience to help me understand why making out is so much fun, but I was glad I had an excuse to end it. It's not like I wanted to marry the guy, and really, with the exception of Chelsea and Tyler, relationships at my age seem like a waste of time. Well, my parents met in high school, but they're my parents and it's just not the same.

So even though I've only kissed two boys, I've had several more try it, and I'm familiar with the signs that it might happen. Ryker Black is difficult to read, but it seems to me like he really wants to kiss me. I mean, he's staring at my lips and breathing hard. Or is that me?

He breaks eye contact first, spinning around to write something down on a sheet of paper. Hopping off the desk, he hands me the paper, tells me it's my locker number and combination, and opens the door, making me think I imagined the whole thing.

Chapter 5

Everything is better after a grueling workout. My head is clearer. I remember the true reason I'm here, and the enigma of Ryker Black is not it. There's just no room for someone like him, who demands all my focus and energy. But when I'm out on the mountain with some of the best junior ski racers in the world, sprinting through a dryland ski course as fast as I can, the only thoughts in my head are *faster, higher, stronger.* A dryland ski course is when gates are set up on a steep slope, just like training when there's snow except instead of wearing skis, we're on our own two feet, running down the hill and trying to take the best angles and turns through the gates in order to maintain momentum, as close as we can get to when we're skiing.

Lia Moretti was at the base of the mountain when Ryker dropped me off in his pickup. All the pickups I've been in before are old and beat up; I didn't even know luxury pickup trucks existed until I slid into the leather cushions in Ryker's passenger seat. He took us to a drive-through, the only one in town, he told me, and we had burgers and fries for lunch. After our conversation in his creepy basement office, we barely spoke to each for the next two hours, and he dropped me off thirty minutes early for my first workout.

Lia had been waiting for my arrival, and she showed me around the training lodge and pointed out my ski locker. Apparently Stark students have their own ski lodge and individual ski lockers. Ingrid said that Ryker was like royalty, but I'm starting to feel like all Stark students are in that league. Ingrid didn't ask about what went down with Ryker, but she did stick to my side during the workout.

Oh, and we didn't get to ride the lift up either. Up and down for nearly two hours with hardly any rest. I'm going to be sore as hell tomorrow. There's not much talking during the workout, I notice, which I guess isn't surprising given how hard we're working. Still, at Sugarville we'd cheer each other on and shout encouragements. It always helped with morale. Guess that's not the style at Stark, or maybe it's first-day nerves.

But on the bus back to campus, which is only a mile away, I hear people talking about summer training.

"Is the summer training part of the Stark program?" I ask Ingrid.

"Not officially, but pretty much everyone goes. In June we're at Mt. Hood in Oregon for three weeks, then we get July off, and we were just in Patagonia for three weeks. We got a week off before starting dryland here at Stark."

"So, everyone has been skiing all summer?" My heart is racing in mild panic. I'm behind *already*? I've been lifting and cross-training faithfully to diminish any possible disadvantage, and yet, there's no way I'll be able to afford flying around the world to find snow in the summer months. That's most certainly not part of the scholarship. Not to mention, I want my summers at home.

Ingrid gives me a funny look. "Yeah, why? Roxie, everyone at Stark does summer training. Like, you don't get to this level if you're not at the Mt. Hood and Patagonia sessions every summer. We can't afford to be off skis for six months straight."

I give her a hard look.

She smiles and shrugs. "Unless you're Roxie Slade, of course. But we all know you don't go to the summer training blocks. Most of us met there before Stark. The programs start at age ten."

Sighing, I shake it off. Yeah, most of the Sugarville Academy kids go to summer ski camps, and even Brad, Tyler and Chelsea go to Mt. Hood in Oregon each summer for two weeks, but they always made it sound like it was more fun than real training. I never felt like I was missing a training opportunity. Of course, they weren't there at the same time as the Stark kids. The three of them always came back with stories of new adventures, and seemed to get into the most trouble. They drank for the first time out there, and went skiing naked one night. I'm pretty sure that's where Brad lost his virginity. It sounded like a huge party to me, and a waste of money.

With the Moretti siblings as coaches, I doubt Stark skiers get up to any shenanigans on the training trips. Besides, we're away from home the entire school year, so it's not a novelty.

Ingrid's not in my dorm, but she asks if I'll meet her at DH for dinner, and I'm more than happy to have someone to sit with this time. Ryker said he wouldn't "approach me" on campus, which made it sound like I've got a disease, but at least that means I can eat without drama. I'm not sure where I stand with Monica. Her reaction last night was not promising of a future friendship.

But she's in our room when I come back from my shower, and it looks like she's ready to talk.

"Are you okay?" That's the first thing she asks.

"Shouldn't I be asking you that question? I haven't seen you in twenty-four hours. Where were you last night?"

"I slept over at a friend's dorm. I'm fine."

Studying her to see if she's enemy or ally, I ask, "Why did you stay with your friend? Boyfriend?"

She giggles then, and I start to think we'll be okay. "No, Misha is just on the figure skating team with me. He likes boys." Right, so there is some truth to Ryker's statement about the handbook rules being meaningless. Monica slept over in a guy's dorm room, and she doesn't strike me as a rule-breaker.

"So, did you get locked out of the building?"

Her eyes widen. "No! Did you? Where did you sleep?" Monica's voice is shrill.

"Relax, I slept here, in my bed. My card wouldn't open the door at first, but then Ryker let me in and it reactivated this morning. I think he just wanted to show me how powerful he is."

Monica visibly relaxes. "Ryker asked me to stay with Misha after you left. I thought it was because he wanted me to stay away from you, like maybe it was a punishment for you to stay alone in the room your first night. Now I wonder if he was planning on keeping you locked out all night and didn't want me to know in case I tried to rescue you."

Yesterday, I would have been appalled by what she's saying. Now, I totally agree with her. I'm still convinced that Ryker's cray-cray but I'm starting to understand the situation a little better, and maybe even accepting it's not a new-girl joke after all. I'll never really get it, that's for sure.

"So, um, I heard you hung out with Ryker today," Monica says a few minutes later after I've thrown some clothes on. "You should really start applying lotion after you shower, by the way. Your skin is going to start flaking off, I swear."

"Yes ma'am," I say with a salute. "You heard I hung out with Ryker, huh? Is this place gossip-y or what?"

"Ingrid told me. We're friends."

"Aha! That's why she was so nice to me today, isn't it?"

"Maybe. She likes you, though."

"She tried to explain some things to me about Ryker. It doesn't all make sense to me, but I think I'll try my best not to piss him off."

Monica grins. "That is very good to hear. I thought I'd be losing another roommate with your attitude last night."

I decide not to tell her about my discussion with Ryker, the rules he listed for me, and our arrangement to meet once a week. It just feels like something I'm supposed to keep to myself. Besides, it will only give Monica anxiety, and so far I think it's a situation I can handle.

When we get to DH, the place is packed with students. Monica tells me that everyone has arrived now, since classes start in two days. No one has mentioned classes to me yet. It's been all about training. I don't even have my schedule.

After filling our trays, Monica leads me to a table where two guys are already sitting. They both stand up to greet us.

"I'm Misha Vans," the one with a trendy haircut says and puts out his hand. He has a very thick Russian accent. At least I think it's Russian.

"Liam Briarwell," the taller of the two, with a ponytail, says and takes my hand. No accent, as far as I can tell. It's becoming unusual to meet Americans at Stark. "We're on the skate team with Monica, and we're roommates."

It's all so formal, I almost giggle. "Roommates, huh? So whose bed did she sleep in last night?"

When I glance over at Monica, bright red is creeping up her neck. Interesting. As we all sit down, Liam informs me that he just arrived this morning, so she slept in his bed last night.

I'm excited to finally enjoy the food at Stark without interruption when a loud voice announces itself.

"Hey!" Ingrid says grumpily. "You were supposed to meet me in the entry!" She plops down next to me and gives me a fake glare.

"Oh shit, sorry Ingrid," I say sincerely. I feel like a jerk.

"She was distracted," Misha says. "Poor thing was traumatized after her experience at DH yesterday."

Oh, great. So he witnessed it, or heard about it. No one asks what he means, which means Ingrid and Liam must know as well.

"Oh, give her a break, Ingrid," Monica says. "I texted you we'd be at the table. I know you weren't waiting for her."

Ingrid smirks. "Just wanted to see if she was intentionally trying to ditch me. I'm not the only one interested in her loyalties."

The table goes silent for a moment at her words.

"I still can't believe you chose *us* over the posse," Misha loud-whispers, glancing over his shoulder.

"The what?" I ask, confused.

Ingrid reaches over and slaps Misha on the back of the head. "Dumbass, she didn't know that's what she was doing."

"She doesn't even know what the posse is," Monica adds, also speaking quietly.

Liam puts his fork down. "You didn't tell her?"

"I only had a few minutes to bring her up to speed, and besides, doesn't it seem like the kind of thing you just *know* or figure out on your own pretty quickly? I mean, look at them," Monica says, gesturing to the table Ryker sat at yesterday, "they just emanate status and coolness."

I look over at the table where the three girls I met the first day are seated with Sven Teslow and another guy I haven't met yet, though I recognize him as the other guy with Player and Ryker who helped moved Monica's stuff yesterday. Ryker isn't with them. I'll admit, they are probably the most beautiful people in the room, but I'm still lost.

"Someone want to tell me what the posse is?" I ask.

Liam looks around before speaking. It's crowded but loud enough in here that I doubt anyone's listening or can hear us.

"This year, it's Sven Teslow, Player Westby, Cody Tremblay, Aspen Davies, Winter Lovett, Telluride Valentini, and Petra Hoffman." Liam lists off the names slowly and reverently.

"And Ryker, obviously," Misha adds.

"Obviously," Ingrid echoes.

I shake my head and take a sip of milk. "That's a list of names, guys, and totally doesn't explain why you call them the posse. Do they tell you to call them that or something? What does it mean?"

"Well, no one *tells* us to call them that, it just *is*," Monica explains. "The people are different every year, usually a mix of juniors and seniors, with the exception of Ryker, of course, who's been in it, well, always, I guess. Right?" She turns to Liam for confirmation.

"Yeah, kind of."

Ingrid finally gets to the point. "The posse is the people who matter the most at Stark. They're the best athletes, come from legacy, have loads of money, and are usually hot."

Misha adds, "Sometimes there's someone who doesn't quite have it all, but is like, so exceptional in one area, that it's cool. Like Abigail Drover, our freshman year? Figure skater who was gorgeous and rich but only made the podium at the national level. Never really broke into the world scene."

Right, and they think I was going to break into that little circle? I'm hardly even on the national scene yet and as far as legacy and money go, I don't run in those elite circles.

The four of them go on about who was in the posse each year since they started as seventh or eighth graders. I recognize a lot of the names, and yeah, they are all those athletes who make it big for more than just their athletic feats. Charisma, connections, looks, I guess it all matters for that level of fame. Me, I just want to race fast. It's hard to imagine what the future holds after even this year. I always assumed I'd try to get a ski scholarship at the University of Vermont or somewhere in New England, but now that I'm at Stark, making *the team* – the U.S. National Team – seems like a real option. Most of the alpine ski racers here forgo college to race for their national team, wherever that may be. I'm not there yet. Not even close. And who knows if that's what I'd want, even if I had the option?

"So, Roxie, why'd you walk the other way?" Liam asks. I've only been half-listening, and I don't know what he's talking about.

"Huh?"

"Ryker invited you to his table, girl," Ingrid fills me in. "That was your *in* to the posse. You won't be getting another."

"Why would I want to be in the posse?" It just sounds like Stark's version of popular people.

The four of them stare at me like I just asked why I would want to ski on a powder day. "What's the point?" I add.

"You're not just set for high school if you're in with them," Liam tells me. "You're set for life. If you think it's just another high school popularity thing, you're wrong. It's much bigger than that."

"Damn straight," Misha adds with a nod.

I'm feeling mighty irritated. In twenty-four hours I've had way too many people telling me what to do and why it matters. I just want to ski. Fast and often. If I get to do it with the best, even better. For free? Definitely. But all this crap about a posse and rules and world domination is just driving me nuts. Sighing, I stand up and head over to the fro yo machine. I need a break.

My legs are already aching and I know I'm going to need another bedtime snack with the workout we did. I wonder if there's a convenience store in walking distance, or if I'm allowed to take stuff from DH. And who do I even ask about that kind of thing? Ryker? As I'm filling up a cone, the air in DH seems to shift. The loud voices dim to a softer buzz, and I can sort of feel heads turning around me. I've learned enough to take a wild guess about what's going on, but as soon as my cone is topped off, I let my gaze drift to the entry, where Ryker is walking in with Player.

For some reason, I expect him to look my way, acknowledge me somehow, but he just nods at a few people as he makes his way to the food line. After the drama from last night, I'd thought he'd seek me out, at least to see where I sat tonight, but he doesn't even glance at Monica or the others at our table when he walks past. I'm oddly disappointed. Perhaps our conversation and time together today didn't mean much to him; I guess it was just "work" keeping the new girl under wraps.

Monica and her friends were mistaken. He didn't want me in the posse; I didn't miss a chance at anything because I never had it. I'm just an unknown, and that requires a little more attention than the average student for the Stark mafia boss. So why am I not relieved that it's nothing more? Doesn't this mean I'm free and clear to be a normal student, like I wanted?

Chapter 6

The next few weeks go kind of like I originally thought they would. We train *hard*. Weights, running, biking, agility, hill sprints, and more jumps and squats than I've ever done in my entire life. It's both exhausting and exhilarating; I love going to bed at night knowing that there's no way I could have pushed my body any harder. And then waking up in the morning with sore muscles; it means I'm getting stronger.

I keep thinking I'll stop having constant muscle aches as my body adjusts, but Rocco and Lia never back off; they just keep adding more difficult agility drills, and increasing pounds on the weight machines. I love working hard, but I can't continue going at this rate. The first snow can't come soon enough, when I'll finally get a chance to use this strength I'm building.

The coolest thing is working out with girls who can kick my ass. Petra and Ingrid dominate all the workouts, and the rest of us just try to keep up. I started out as one of the weakest, at least for an upper classman. A couple of the freshmen could outlift me and beat me on agility courses. But I'm improving fast -- I just hope the same thing happens when we get on skis.

Classes are more intense than I expected, but that's mainly because we do all the school work in about half the time of normal high school students. There's minimal assigned homework. Most school work is done during class hours, with a very specific lesson or project. Occasionally we read or write a paper during the class period. There are no time-wasting assignments. We learn what we have to learn to pass the standardized tests; as far as I can tell, no one is here for academics.

There's not much downtime, which is how I like it. In Ashfield, I had to spend time driving to and from the mountain and occasionally I'd help out at the general store. There was plenty of sitting around with my friends during and between workouts. Here, I train nearly twice as much as I did back home, but there's no wasted time in the car since everything's close, and no hallway time, or leisurely sitting-around-chatting-and-listening-to-music time. With the exception of the short shuttle ride to the mountain, eating meals at DH is the only real social time we get, and I've gotten into the routine of eating with Monica, Ingrid, Misha and Liam. Or just Ingrid if the skaters are at practice.

It's been nearly a month and I still haven't seen my friends skate yet. With a few minutes to spare before hitting the weight room, I head over to the arena to see if I can catch them on the ice.

The cold air hits me when I open the doors, and as I'm making my way over to the stadium benches, my eyes trained on the rink, a flood of guys streams out of the locker room. It's the hockey team, I can tell right away by their physiques, which are bulkier than any of the figure skaters. A few eye me curiously as I pass them, but then I'm drawn back to the rink, where a couple is practicing a routine. At least, that's what they seem to be doing, given that the music coordinates with their movements.

At first, I don't realize it's Monica and Liam. I know they are a pairs team, but the couple on the rink looks like the Olympians I've watched on television, not the friends I eat with every day at DH. Their movements are so smooth, so graceful, so *perfect*. It's no wonder Monica has a crush on Liam, because the way he guides her, lifts her, glides alongside her, is beyond romantic. It's beautiful. Does he not see it? Or does he prefer guys, like Misha? Perhaps all skating couples share a certain chemistry on the ice that doesn't necessarily translate off of it. But I've seen them together, too, and I wish I could give Liam a little shove, or better yet, slap some sense into him.

A presence at my side breaks me from my plotting. Glancing over, I'm surprised to find Cody Tremblay sitting down next to me. We've never spoken, but since he's a member of the posse, everyone knows who he is. He did show up that first day at my dorm with Ryker and helped Monica move her stuff in, but we didn't actually meet.

"Hey Roxie, I'm Cody." He says it warmly, and I don't detect a threat there.

"Yeah, I know who you are, Cody Tremblay." I glance over at him and he laughs quietly. He's wearing a flannel shirt and a beanie over his shaggy dark hair. He must have stayed back a year or perhaps two, because he doesn't look like a teenager. "What's up?" If he's speaking to me, he must have a reason.

"Just saying hi, introducing myself. I wanted to finally meet the girl who's got Ryker's panties in a twist."

My eyes practically bulge out of my head and then I laugh. The words *panties* and *Ryker* sound ridiculous together. "He's over it, I'm sure. I haven't even spoken to him since my first day."

Cody studies me curiously, a secret smile playing on his lips. "So, what brings you to Stark Arena?" He leans forward and rests his elbows on his knees, like he's settling in for a cozy conversation.

For a moment here, the thought occurs to me that Ryker is finally following through on his plans to meet with me once a week, and he's sent his buddy to tell me when and where. But that's a stupid thought. Why would he send Cody, first of all? And second, why now? It seems to me he's either forgotten all about it, decided I wasn't any "danger" to Stark, or the whole situation really was an attempt at a prank, but everyone decided it was too much effort to follow through. I haven't decided yet. The truth is, even though no one says his name much, I still sense that Ryker runs things around here. It's impossible to deny.

"I'm spying on my friends," I finally answer, nodding to the rink. I'm unsure why Cody is talking to me. But there's no one else around, so maybe he really does just want to meet me without an audience. Without Ryker Black, in particular. Hmmm... I glance at Cody again.

"First time at the rink? I've never seen you here before."

"First time. And I didn't even recognize them at first. They're amazing."

Cody nods, and we watch Liam and Monica in silence for a few minutes. We're in the shadows, and I don't think anyone's noticed us.

"Are you coming to the dance tonight?" he asks when the song ends.

"I'm not sure. Maybe." Ingrid hates dances, and wants me to boycott it in favor of a movie night. Monica and Misha want me to go to the dance with them. I'm not sure where Liam stands.

"You should come," Cody tells me. "We don't get to have fun outside of sports very often around here. But the dances are always a good time."

It doesn't sound like he's asking me on a date, but it still makes me uneasy. He's not interested in me like that, is he? Nah, just being friendly to the new girl.

"I'll probably check it out," I admit. I'm too curious about the first social event at Stark since I've arrived to completely ditch it. "It might not be as much fun as dancing in my dorm room with my roommate, but I'll give it a try." Monica and I quickly discovered that we share a guilty love for Taylor Swift, and occasionally we like to start the day spinning around our room like idiots.

"Oh, really?" Cody's eyebrows rise in interest and I shrug. Sometimes I accidentally say something that can be interpreted as flirting, so I tell him I've got to get to the weight room but that it was good to meet. He doesn't offer to walk me out or anything, which is good. It's not that I'm worried about Ryker's rules; if anything, I think he was just messing with me that day, but I'm truly not interested in having a boyfriend, even a cutie like Cody. Besides, he's in the posse, and that would probably make it even more complicated.

Our team captain, Petra Hoffman, doesn't seem to be my biggest fan, and I don't want to give her any reason to take notice of me, aside from being her teammate. I don't think I've done anything to make her dislike me, but she's even ruder to me than she is to everyone else on the team, and shoots me these pointed, mean looks. I try to avoid her.

I actually lied about needing to get over to the weight room, and I've got a few minutes to kill, so I call Chelsea. She doesn't answer, so I try Brad, who picks up right away.

"Hey, Rox, how's it going?" The sound of his voice is always comforting. I talk to my friends almost every day, even if it's just for a minute or two between classes. My parents require routine evening phone calls each night after dinner.

"Just headed over to pump some iron. You guys have a game today?" Brad and Tyler play soccer in the fall. Unlike Stark, Sugarville Academy has soccer in the fall and lacrosse in the spring for skiers who still want to play other sports in the off-season.

"We just had a quick workout today. Coach let us off early."

"Nice, any plans?"

He hesitates. "Just hanging out with some people."

I roll my eyes. Brad always tries to dance around telling me that he's hooking up with someone. "Uh-huh," I say knowingly. "What *some* people?"

He sighs. "A girl," he admits. He never wants to talk about his girls. And there are many. Whatever. "So, what's happening at Stark? Any signs of snow?"

"It's only October second, Brad," I remind him. "But it gets damn cold at night, so maybe soon. I just went to see Monica and Liam at practice, and they were incredible. They were doing a pairs routine and they looked like professionals."

"They practically are, aren't they?"

"True. Still, it was unreal watching them. Monica is this gentle, unassuming creature most of the time -- well, except when she's listening to Taylor Swift -- but damn, on the ice she's magical."

"That's awesome, Rox. I can't wait to meet your friends. Stark sounds like it's busting at the seams with talent."

We knew it was before I came here. But now that I'm living it, seeing it every day, getting to know these teenage superstars, it feels more real. Stark was always this far-off abstract phenomenon before I arrived.

"I wish there was a good time for you guys to come visit," I say with a sigh. "We pretty much train straight through Thanksgiving. I'm coming home for Christmas though, even if it's just for a few days," I declare. I haven't raised the subject with Ingrid or the coaches yet, and I need to. I'm pretty sure most of the international students stay here to train, but I can easily train when I'm home, if that's an issue. It's right at the beginning of the racing season, which means we can't take any time off the snow.

We talk for a few more minutes, and I tell Brad to stay out of trouble. He's a good guy, but he tends to do whatever he wants. Tyler and Chelsea will keep an eye on him without me there, as long as they aren't too wrapped up in each other, that is.

The weight room is buzzing with energy this afternoon, and I quickly discern that my teammates are excited about the dance. With the exception of Ingrid, who scowls when I encourage her to go with me.

"You would've liked it at Sugarville High then," I tell her.

"Oh? Why's that?"

"No one went to our school dances. Sometimes we'd make an appearance, but usually it was just a good cover for a big party."

"Yes, but was there dancing at these parties? What did you all do?"

She hops off the leg machine after finishing her set and I slide into her place, but drop the weight by thirty pounds. "What most teenagers do at parties, I imagine."

Ingrid continues looking at me. "Well, what do most teenagers do at parties?" she asks.

I wait until I'm done with the set to respond. "No partying at Stark then, I take it?" If there is, I certainly haven't heard about it. "Or back home in Austria?"

"No, not really," she says. "So, lots of binge drinking, drugs and sex? Like the movies?"

I can't help but laugh at her question. "Sure, I guess. But that's not everyone. Not me, at least."

"That's good to know." The deep voice behind me holds a note of amusement. It's the first time he's spoken to me in a month, and I'm not about to fall over him, as if I've been waiting for this opportunity. Even if I have been waiting.

Instead, I give Ryker a dismissive look and move to the next machine.

When he doesn't follow, and no one except Ingrid seems to notice our interaction, I sneak a peek behind me as I adjust the weight on the machine. He's watching me with a frown, indecision written on his face. Up until now, he's looked so confident and sure, it's nice to see a moment of vulnerability. Or perhaps he's deciding whether or how to make my life hell. He said he wouldn't approach me, and he did. He said we'd meet once a week, and we haven't. I can't decide if I like him to keep his distance or if I want to get to know him better. It seems my life would be a lot easier if he stayed away.

Chapter 7

"I can't believe you talked me into this," I grumble as Monica tugs me along the sidewalk.

She's outfitted me in an emerald dress that is at least two sizes too small and convinced me to wear my hair down, which I *never* do. When I told her I was planning to wear jeans and a tee shirt to the dance, she turned into this feisty little woman I hadn't seen yet. It was so fascinating, watching her take charge of my wardrobe, hair and makeup, that I didn't protest. Plus, I was still sort of in awe after watching her on the ice.

"The dress is not too small. It fits you perfectly. I ordered it online and didn't know the sizes ran big, so you can have it. Besides, that color matches your eyes, and by the way, you really need to wear your hair down more often. I had no idea you had streaks of red in there. It's awesome."

"They're not red," I protest. "It just looks that way sometimes in the light."

"Oh, they're red all right. It's quite striking, Roxie. You don't have the skin tone of a redhead, it's sort of exotic."

I roll my eyes. "Why are they having it at the Stark Springs Resort and Spa, anyway? And are you sure people will be dressed up like us? I don't remember hearing about this being a formal. *Is* it a formal?" An unwelcome nervousness is seeping into me, and I'm not sure why. I rarely get nervous unless it's a ski race. It must be this dress.

"The dances are always at the Resort," Roxie tells me. "It's not very far. When the weather's bad, they sometimes have shuttles to and from, since not very many students have cars."

We're off campus now, walking along Main Street. I haven't spent much time in downtown Stark, but it's a charming place, with restaurants and shops. It almost feels more welcoming and less intimidating than the buildings at school. Friendlier.

I'm surprised to find men in suits at the door who check our names on a little iPad before allowing us inside. I mean really, it's not like there are many, if any other teenagers in Stark who might crash the dance. Maybe I shouldn't be surprised, though. The only thing at Stark that's been more or less what I expected is the workouts.

Monica gives me a tentative sidelong glance when we step inside the dance hall. It's nearly empty, with the exception of the DJ and a few other students standing around. "Sorry," she says, embarrassed. "I like to be early. Most people won't be here for another hour."

I shrug. "Actually, it's pretty cool we have the dance floor to ourselves." I take her hand, and she shakes her head in protest. "I know you love this song." She won't admit it, but Monica has a thing for Justin Bieber. I've seen her iTunes library and caught her reading gossip articles about him online.

Once I start moving, Monica gets into it. It's no surprise the girl can *dance*. She's one of those people who has a body that just knows what to do, no matter what song is playing. Even in our confined dorm room, she works it like she's on a stage or something. I find myself trying to emulate her, and it's not long before we forget we're not alone here. As the songs switch from one to the next, the dance floor begins to fill up, and before I know it, there's barely any space to move.

Liam and Misha have joined us, and I'm now dancing in a small circle with three of the top junior figure skaters in the world. They are hands down the best dancers in the room, especially as far as the guys go. Most dudes are just trying to find a girl they can wrap themselves around and hide behind as they pretend to dance but really just grind and have sexual fantasies. No one's approached me yet, and I'm thankful for it, though wondering if there's something wrong with me. Nearly everyone on the dance floor is paired off. Perhaps my figure skating friends intimidate everyone. The thought makes me giggle.

And then I notice Monica glancing at Liam every few seconds and decide he needs to get a clue. I move between them, so I'm facing Misha, and put my arms around his neck.

"Is Liam taking the hint?" I ask Misha.

He grins, glancing over my shoulder. "Yep."

"Excellent."

I wonder if it's harder or easier for skating partners to decipher attraction signals, since they're always embracing and touching and stuff at practice. Liam's either mistaking Monica's signals as something else, or he's in denial.

Misha has no shame as he takes me in his arms and coordinates our movements. Wow. He exudes sexuality when he moves, and he's making me feel the same way, despite our lack of mutual attraction. I'm having trouble keeping up with him, thankful that I talked my way out of wearing heels in favor of high top Chuck Taylors. The room is getting hotter with all these moving bodies, and I can feel sweat forming on my lower back. Sheesh, even the dances at Stark are like a sporting event.

Misha's movements come to a stop in the middle of a song, and he drops his hands and steps away as if I burned him. I open my mouth to ask what's up, but strong hands wrap around my waist, and Misha disappears into the crowd.

"I didn't know you could dance like that." Ryker's voice is in my ear, his lips inches from my cheek. It's difficult to hear over the music, but I don't protest when he guides my hips in front of him. He has rhythm, I'll give him that.

When the song changes a moment later, I spin around, wanting to see his face. His head is down, his eyes in shadow, but standing there in the darkness, the occasional strobe light flashing across his face, he's all I can see. The people around us blur, and I don't know if it's the heavy beat disorienting my thoughts or the sense of anonymity on the crowded dance floor, but I boldly place my hands around his neck and step in close, so our bodies are almost touching.

He lets me.

Ryker's hands settle just below my hips, and I sense that he's exercising restraint with a light touch. Possessive, but gentle. He watches me for a moment and then pulls me closer, his head dropping so it's almost resting on mine. We're nearly flush against each other now, swaying as one.

Dancing this way with a boy should be awkward and uncomfortable, but it's not. Not at all. Ryker doesn't seem like a stranger in this moment. He seems like someone I've known for a very long time. It's almost magical, the way we're glued together, and I've got no anxiety about what it means, or where it goes.

That all changes when the song switches to a slow one. Slow ones mean something, and I pull away slightly. I'm dazed, and Ryker's expression is determined. It seems to be his default expression.

Keeping a hand on my hip, he guides me off the dance floor, and as we emerge from the crowd, I feel the weight of stares. We pass Monica and Liam, who are slow dancing together, and that makes me smile. Though neither of them are focused on the other. Instead, they are watching me with undisguised interest. Monica's eyes hold a question but all I can do is shrug. I have no idea what I'm doing, but whatever it is, I can't seem to help myself. Aside from the comment at the gym earlier, this is the first interaction I've had with Ryker in nearly a month, and I'm not too ashamed to admit that I'm reveling in it.

When I see he's guiding us toward the posse, I hesitate. Petra is leaning against a windowsill, glaring at me, and looking stunning in a white strapless dress. Cody has hopped onto the window ledge and flashes a knowing smirk when our eyes meet. My eyes narrow in response. If this was some sort of set-up, I'm going to be pissed. He did check to see if I was coming earlier, and now he's looking very pleased with himself.

Winter, Aspen and Sven are chatting but their conversation stops as soon as we approach. Ryker nods at his friends and grabs a coat.

"Where's your jacket?" he asks me.

"Why?"

His eyes flash and he begins to steer me away from the group. "Remember the compromise we made? You've been off the hook, but I want to have our meeting. Right now."

The usual note of threat in his tone is wrapped in something else, and the piece of me still lost in the moment on the dance floor wants it to be a promise. A promise of what, I'm not so sure.

This is when I would normally protest and resist his demanding attitude. But for some inexplicable reason, I want to go with him. He's irritating as all hell, but probably the most intriguing person I've ever met. I mean really, where does he get off acting like, well, like the prince of Stark Springs?

Ingrid's description that first day sounded ludicrous, but now I realize it may have been spot on.

Grabbing the jacket I threw in the corner when we first arrived, I catch Monica's eye and tilt my head, mouthing that I'm leaving. She just nods. No questions asked. Hopefully he's not plotting something evil.

A valet has already pulled up Ryker's pickup; he hands Ryker the keys as soon as we exit, nodding and calling him "Mr. Black." It's hard not to roll my eyes or laugh.

"Where are we going?" I ask as we pull away.

Ryker glances over at me, his eyes trailing down my body and back up before answering. "I should bring you home. You broke a rule."

Letting out a huff, I cross my arms. "What rule? Besides, it's not like you've been meeting with me every week like you said you would, so I figured all the BS was moot."

His eyebrows rise in amusement. "BS? It isn't BS, Roxanne. And it's not moot."

I look out the window and notice a few snowflakes in the lamplight. The first sign of snow is always awe-inspiring, and I can't help my gasp of appreciation. The white flakes float downward and disappear into the black street.

"I didn't know it was going to snow tonight," I whisper, my fingers on the window as if I can reach out and catch the flakes.

"It just hit freezing. Did you walk all the way over to the Resort in that dress?"

"It's like, less than a mile, Ryker, relax."

His fists clench the wheel and he murmurs, "There's another rule you're dangerously close to breaking."

My eyes are going to get tired from rolling them so much around this guy.

"What was the other rule I allegedly broke, anyway?"

I notice that Ryker is driving past campus, so I guess he decided not to take me back to the dorm.

"Don't pretend you don't know. It seemed to me you were doing it on purpose. Just to get to me."

I laugh. "Do you mean dancing with Misha? You know we're not into each other like that, right?"

"Maybe not, but it looked like the two of you were putting on a show. Everyone was watching. If that wasn't an attempt to get guys looking at you, I don't know what is."

My jaw drops. What an asshole. "I was just dancing with my friend! You couldn't even call what most of the people there were doing 'dancing.' It was just an excuse to grope people, from what I could tell. At least I was dancing."

Ryker just shakes his head and I can't tell if he's frustrated, angry or amused.

"Besides, *you* danced with me," I add after a moment.

"I'm an exception to the rule," he says easily. Of course he is.

He pulls onto a dirt driveway, and my stomach churns with unease. "Where are we going?" I ask again.

"My house."

"Your house? You don't live in the dorms?"

He gives me an odd look. "I have a dorm room. But I'm from Stark, so I sometimes stay at my house."

"Why are we going to your house?" The suspicion in my voice is obvious.

He glances over at me, his face blank. "You can't guess?"

Now I'm not so much afraid, but embarrassed. Does he think I want to hook up with him? From one dance? Sure, it was a hot dance, but I hardly even know him. If anything, I've given him every indication that I don't like him and I'm not interested in him like that. Haven't I? Right, okay, there was that almost-kiss in his office and I guess there's an undeniable attraction between us, but does he seriously think he can just bring me to his house and I'll jump all over him?

"Take me back to the dance, Ryker," I say through gritted teeth. "I don't want to hook up with you."

A house comes into view then. There are lights leading to a garage and illuminating the front of a modern home with several decks and balconies and huge windows. It's an image suited for a magazine cover, and it wouldn't surprise me in the slightest if it had been featured on HGTV. I'm almost tempted to go inside just to see what it looks like.

Ryker hasn't responded to me yet and when I look over at him, his chest is rising and falling in silent laughter.

"Are you *laughing* at me?" I'm pissed but I'm also pleased. If I had to guess, Ryker Black doesn't laugh very often, and I like that he's doing it with me, even if it's at my expense.

"No. Well, yeah," he admits, still not looking at me. When he drives under a lamp, his smile widens, and I notice for the first time a dimple under his right cheekbone. Oh no, this isn't good. A guy like Ryker Black *cannot* have dimples. It's wrong. And right. *Too* right.

"Damn," I say under my breath. I feel Ryker looking over at me as he hits the garage door button on his visor. It's big enough for four cars, but half of it is filled with outdoor gear. The skis, snowboards, a snowmobile, bikes, and various other toys are neatly arranged, hanging from hooks or set on racks. It's an outdoor enthusiast's dream garage.

I'm still staring out the window when the passenger door opens and I realize Ryker has turned off the engine. He reaches a hand out to me and I almost take it before frowning and gripping my seat belt.

"I told you, take me back. I'm not going in there with you."

Ryker reaches over me, unclicks my seat belt, and pulls it back from my waist. "What if I promise not to try to hook up with you?" He's totally laughing at me and my earlier statement.

Now I'm *really* embarrassed. What was I thinking? Of course Ryker Black doesn't want that with me. He even told me, and Monica confirmed, that he wants to get to know me only because I'm new. I'm an unknown, and apparently, his responsibility to keep in check. I'm only here at his house so he can... what? Make sure I'm not going to murder anyone at Stark? Check to confirm I'm not a drug dealer or addict? I have no idea. It's weird enough I'm already starting to think that his behavior *isn't* super weird.

And I'm even letting him guide me out of the car and into his home. Though his promise eases my nerves, it's a little disappointing that the concept of bringing me here for that purpose is so entertaining to him. Whatever.

"Unless, of course, you change your mind," he adds as he opens the door. "You just let me know. I'm down."

The ease with which he talks about it makes my blood boil. Obviously, bringing girls home for the purpose of making out, or more, is something he does casually and often. Even though Brad has been that way since the eighth grade and it never bothered me, I find it very unsettling that Ryker might be the same way about women and intimacy and relationships, or the lack thereof.

But then I'm standing in the mudroom, and my attention shifts. We're surrounded by wall-to-wall cubbies labeled and filled with outdoor gear ranging from ski goggles to mittens. One wall contains the largest shoe rack I've ever seen in my life. It's not filled with stilettos, but with sneakers, snow boots, ski boots, snowboarding boots, and all manly forms of shoe wear imaginable.

"Do you live here by yourself?" I wonder.

"Mostly. My dad's here sometimes. Not sure where he is at the moment, but he's not in Stark." Ryker's standing at the door to the rest of the house, waiting for me. Once again, he's giving me a look that tells me he's surprised I don't already know everything about his life. Just because he seems to have access to all the details in *my* life, doesn't mean I'm privy to the same info on his.

I follow him to the kitchen and find myself struggling to focus on anything but the unrealness of his home. Yeah, I was told he came from wealth, but this is nothing like the nicer homes in Sugarville or Ashfield. This is the kind of home movie stars live in. People with unlimited amounts of money.

Ryker leans against the kitchen counter and watches me look around. "So," he finally says. "If you don't want to hook up, what do you want to do?"

Chapter 8

My emotions flash from outrage, to satisfaction, and then, admittedly, to lust. Is lust an emotion?

"Well, you never answered my question," I say when I've finally gathered myself. "Why did you bring me here?"

"Come on, Roxanne. Have you ever been to a guy's house, on a Friday night, alone, for any other purpose? I didn't think you were the type to play games. You gave me every green light back at the Resort. If you say you don't want it, we won't go there. But don't pretend you don't know why you're here."

My mouth is hanging open. I just can't quite comprehend the words he's saying. They are beyond insulting. He's stripped me down to an object, a person with no purpose and no qualities except my gender. I think back to what he said about my dancing with Misha. He thinks I was dancing that way because I wanted this kind of thing. For a brief moment, I feel ashamed. I feel like an idiot. A naïve, stupid girl, who understands nothing. But that lasts only an instant. It's Ryker at fault here. Not me.

"I'm out of here." I don't even want a ride. I can't stand another second in the car with this pig. We're only a few minutes from campus, and I've got my Converse on, so I'm fine walking.

I go back the way we came, not pausing to take in the mudroom this time. I'm looking for the button to open the garage door when Ryker pulls me back inside.

"Don't touch me." I'm trying for a confident, controlled tone, but even to my own ears, I sound a little hysterical.

He immediately releases me but as he does, he says, "Please don't go." I think it's the first time I've heard any note of insecurity in his voice, and it gives me pause.

"I'm sorry, Roxanne," he says to my back. "I should have known you were different. I did know it. I do." He's at a loss for words, and that suggests he's actually feeling remorseful. I hope.

"Will you look at me, please? I'm not used to apologizing, and I don't like doing it to the back of your head."

Sighing, I turn around.

"It's fine, Ryker. We clearly have different ideas about, um, this kind of thing, or whatever." Why am I making excuses for him? Why am I the one embarrassed again? "I should go. And I'd rather just walk."

"Let's hang out. We've got pool, foosball, air hockey, movies, whatever."

I look down at my feet. I really should go. He's already told me what he expected tonight, and now he probably just wants to redeem himself. But he sounds so earnest, and besides, why would a guy like him care about redeeming himself to a girl like me?

"Do you never hang out with girls unless you're... you know?"

"Not alone. No."

I ponder that for a moment.

"Roxanne, you don't actually hang out with guys, alone at their homes, without any expectation of hooking up, do you?" He asks it as though it's a rhetorical question.

I think about it. Alone? I guess only with Brad.

"One of my best friends is a guy. Brad has been my friend since kindergarten. And I've hung out with Tyler alone occasionally but he's been in love with my best girlfriend for years. I hang out with guys in groups all the time. There are a few, like you, who would assume it meant more if we were alone, but most just treat me like a buddy. Not one of the guys, exactly, but not like someone they're trying to hook up with either," I explain. It's not something I've ever really thought about.

"Well, this Brad guy wants in your pants, and the other guys just know they don't have a chance, or you've known them for so long you don't know that they're trying to get in your pants. Trust me."

"Not all guys are like you, Ryker," I tell him.

"No guys are like me, Roxanne. But I guarantee you, unless the dude is head over heels for another woman, like this Tyler guy, they want in your pants."

I huff out a breath. This is pointless.

"Or they like guys, like Misha," he adds.

"Whatever." We're not getting anywhere with this, and I'm tired of hearing him talk about getting inside pants. It makes me want to look at his pants and think about what's inside. "Even if that's the case, which it isn't, can't girls be more than just that one thing? Why can't guys also want to just hang out with girls, as friends?"

Ryker studies me for a long moment. I add, "Like the girls you hang out with, Winter, Aspen, Petra, Telluride. I'm sure you don't expect to hook up with them every time you hang out."

"That's usually the assumption if we're alone or I take them somewhere."

I almost choke on my water. "You've hooked up with all of them?"

He shrugs. "That's what I'm saying. It happens and it's no big deal. To them or to me. I can see now that it would be for you. So let's try to pretend you're one of the guys tonight. If you were Player, we'd hit up the pool table. Sven's into table tennis. Cody's obsessed with air hockey, no surprise there."

"Wait, did you tell Cody to ask me to come to the dance tonight?" I'm curious if he's trying to meddle in my life. But Ryker's eyes narrow, and I know I shouldn't have asked.

"You talked to Cody?" He's pissed, and I don't know why. Is the posse really that exclusive? I'm not supposed to talk to any of them?

"Never mind," I say. "Let's hit up this pool table."

Ryker looks reluctant to drop it but eventually he leads me upstairs to an open loft space. After taking in the endless games, I wander over to the floor-to-ceiling windows overlooking Stark Mountain. Though the lights are dim in the loft, it's too dark to see anything out there unless my head is pressed against the glass. The snow is really coming down now.

Feeling Ryker beside me, I ask, "Is it normal for it to snow so hard this time of year? It was in the sixties earlier today."

"It's a little early, but not unusual. The weather comes in fast here. It can be a bluebird day in the morning and a blizzard in the afternoon."

I'm not surprised that Ryker is an excellent pool player. He seems like the kind of guy who's good at everything. We're on our third game when I remember he said he used to ski.

"When did you switch to snowboarding? What made you drop ski racing?" He looks surprised by my question so I add, "You said you used to ski."

Shaking his head, Ryker tells me the most honest thing he's said yet. "Most people think they already know everything about me. And they're too afraid to ask the real questions. You're different, Roxanne."

"Maybe you don't hang out with the right people," I point out. "Not everyone in Ashfield, Vermont knows everything about you. And we're not scared of asking you questions, either."

He doesn't respond to that, but he does answer my original question. "I grew up ski racing, but I always wanted to snowboard. I'd watch the riders on the pipe when we went up the lift, and follow them through the trees on powder days. It looked like so much fun. My parents wouldn't let me learn, though. But eventually I went ahead and learned to snowboard on my own."

We aren't playing anymore, just leaning against the pool table. "How old were you?"

"Twelve."

"How'd you get the equipment? Lessons?"

He glances at me. "I know people."

The way he says it reminds me of Ingrid's words, that he's the mafia boss of winter, and I'm so tempted to ask him about it, but I hold back. For now.

"So you started snowboarding right around when you started at the academy? Which team did you join?"

"I was on the alpine team until my freshman year, and then I switched to snowboarding."

"How'd your parents handle it?"

"My dad didn't like it, but couldn't do much about it. My mom died when I was twelve."

On reflex, I reach out to touch his arm. "I'm sorry, Ryker."

He doesn't say anything more about it and neither of us have much interest in playing pool anymore. It's time for me to go home, I guess, but I'm not ready. I finally feel like I'm getting somewhere with Ryker, even if I don't know where we're going. He's not giving me much, leaving me with more questions than answers, but it's enough. Enough for what? I don't know. I'm afraid if I go home now, I'll never know.

"I lied earlier." His hands are on the pool table and he's leaning forward, looking at me intently on the other side.

"About what?"

"The meetings, and why I brought you here." He pauses before continuing. "That day at the gym, alone in my office with you, I just knew I wanted more of it, and that you wouldn't give it to me freely."

"What do you mean by 'it?'"

"You and me, talking, and no one else around. You didn't want in with my friends, you made that clear." He allows a smile at that, and he looks almost *proud* of me. "And I don't normally associate with Stark girls in any other capacity," he begins to explain but sees me grinning. "What?"

"'Associate with girls in any other capacity?' Who *says* that? We're not at a board meeting or in a courtroom, Ryker."

"I'm trying not to offend your delicate sensibilities."

My hand goes to my face. "You can't be serious," I groan, unable to muffle my laughter now. "Delicate sensibilities?" My chuckles turn into a full belly laugh. Ryker doesn't look amused, at all. "You're not kidding?" I ask, sobering. "This is really how you talk, isn't it?"

"Sometimes, when I'm trying to explain something meaningful and important."

"Sorry," I say, but I'm still kind of grinning. "Continue."

He glares at me. "What I was *trying* to say before I was so rudely interrupted," he begins, and it takes all my strength not to giggle again. What a horrible time to get the giggles. Everything out of his mouth sounds so hilarious to me for some reason. "I wanted time with you. Like this, what we're doing now." He gestures between us. "Hanging out, talking."

"But you didn't follow through," I point out. "Until tonight."

"No, I was able to refrain. Until tonight. And then once I got you in the car I didn't know what to do with you. I didn't want to take you back to the dorms. I wanted to take you to my house. But then, well, it seemed it might be easier if I treated you like any other girl."

"Easier?"

"Less complicated."

"Complicated?" I'm pushing him, but he needs it. He can't get away with being vague about something like this.

"We can't be anything, Roxanne. You can't be anyone to me, aside from another student, another girl."

His expression doesn't match his words. He's looking at me like I am someone more to him already. But I sense that now isn't the time to push further.

"Do you want to watch a movie?" I ask instead. If he wants to hang out with me, I'm down. As long as I keep getting to see this side of him, the one that talks to me for real and isn't trying to prove something, make a point, or boss me around.

"Yeah, let's go downstairs." He smiles as he takes my hand. It's not a smirk or laughter, just a pleasant, natural expression, and it makes my entire body go warm. Though hand-holding signifies something romantic, I can't deny that he did just kind of admit he's interested in me in a different way. He might not realize that's what he was telling me, but that's how I interpreted it. I let him guide me down two flights of stairs and into a home theater. Tyler's house has something like this, with the theater-style chairs and giant television.

We decide on a comedy, Ryker makes some popcorn, and before we settle in, he runs upstairs to change out of his slacks and button-down. I'm tempted to ask to borrow something more comfortable, like I would if I were at Tyler's or Brad's place, but I'm not there yet with Ryker. So when he tosses me a pair of sweatpants and a long-sleeved shirt, I'm pleasantly surprised. He makes hot chocolate while I change, and though the clothes hang off of me, they're cozy.

The theater seats provide a natural buffer between us, which is probably a good thing. It's unclear what we're doing together here, at this point, and so far we've managed to avoid any awkward moments, despite the undefined territory we're treading.

I must doze during the movie because at some point later in the night, I wake to Ryker murmuring my name and touching my cheek. The credits are rolling, and my mind is fuzzy. I'm not sure if we have a conversation about it, or if I just nod in agreement, but the next thing I know, Ryker is tucking me into bed in a guest room. He kisses me on the forehead, and the moment is so sweet, so tender, that I'm convinced it's a dream.

Chapter 9

Monica doesn't ask any questions when I show up the next morning in our dorm room. When I woke up at Ryker's house, I was nervous about how he would react. But he continued to be attentive and warm as we ate breakfast together and he drove me back to the dorms. It's our first day off from training – the entire campus has the day off – and part of me hoped he'd ask about my plans for the day. But he didn't say anything about when I might see him again, and he pulled away, shifting back to cold and distant, as soon as we got onto campus.

"Ingrid wants to go hiking," Monica informs me. "She's coming over in ten minutes to pick us up."

"Us?"

"Yep. I figured you'd be back by now. Actually, I thought you'd be earlier, but you've still got time to change." She eyes my outfit, and I remember that I'm still wearing Ryker's sweats, folded over three times, and his shirt.

"It's not what you think," I tell her. "We just played pool and watched a movie and then I fell asleep."

Monica looks away, as if I've hurt her feelings. "You don't have to tell me what happened, Roxie, but don't lie."

"What? I'm not lying. Why would I?"

Monica shrugs, turning away as I change into workout clothes. "Bring a bathing suit. We're hiking to the hot springs."

That puts me in a better mood. I'd heard about this hike to the Stark hot springs, and wondered when I'd get the chance to check it out. Leave it to Stark students to go on a long hike on our day off.

"Seriously, Monica, why do you think I'm lying?" When she doesn't answer, I turn around and she points up in a circle, reminding me that she thinks our room is bugged. I just shake my head, irritated.

Ingrid picks us up in her roommate's car. Her roommate, a cross country skier, is doing what normal kids do on a day off and sitting inside watching television. I let Monica take shotgun but as soon as we're in the car and I've said a quick hello to Ingrid, I'm back to grilling Monica.

"Okay, why did you call me a liar?"

Monica doesn't answer right away, and Ingrid butts in. "Whoa, what's going on? Roommate tiff?"

Monica answers first, her voice delicate, as usual. "Roxie had this hot dance with Ryker last night, and then they left together and she didn't come home until this morning. He dropped her off."

"Okaaay…" Ingrid says hesitantly as she drives through campus.

I answer Ingrid's unasked question. "I told Monica we only played pool and watched a movie and then I fell asleep at his house and she called me a liar."

"She was wearing Ryker's clothes," Monica asserts, as if it proves her point.

"Children, children," Ingrid mocks us. "Let's discuss this."

There's a minute of uncomfortable silence before Ingrid carefully turns to Monica at a stop sign. "Why do you think Roxie's lying?"

I can't see Monica's face because I'm sitting directly behind her, but she doesn't sound mad. "It just doesn't make sense, you know that, Ingrid. You remember how he treated Olga, and it's like that with the posse too, only he at least acknowledges them on campus and socializes with them at DH."

Monica turns to face me. "I don't know why you would lie, Roxie -- maybe you're embarrassed or you don't trust me. But I find it very hard to believe Ryker took you back to his house in Stark just to hang out, then let you sleep there, in his clothes, and drove you back to the dorms late this morning."

"Well, it's true. You don't have to believe me."

Monica looks like she might cry. "Roxie, I just don't want the same thing to happen to you that happened to Olga, okay?" Her voice cracks and I'm unprepared for her breakdown. Tears begin to fill her eyes and she turns back around in her seat, wiping them before they fall.

Ingrid pats Monica on the leg and I'm totally confused. What do I say to that? I don't even know what she means.

Ingrid saves me. "Olga and Ryker hooked up every now and then. We think it started freshman year, but she didn't talk about it much. The thing is, Ryker doesn't want girls to talk about it when he's with them. He doesn't like gossip. I mean, it's not like you can't tell your friends," she adds, like she's making a point, "but he keeps that kind of thing under wraps. Anyway, we always knew when Olga had been with Ryker, and not just because Monica was her roommate. She'd be so happy for like, days afterward, and then so bummed. It was pretty annoying, but we never said anything to her about it. Well, did *you* talk to her about it?" Ingrid asks Monica.

"Maybe once, I told her that she shouldn't go off with him anymore. It wasn't ever going to be exclusive for him. He only ever took her to his dorm room on campus though. I don't think she ever went to his house. That's how it usually goes, I think. Except for maybe the posse. They hang at his house a lot."

I'm starting to feel sicker by the second as the girls talk. Ryker didn't hide it from me, how he is, but they're making it sound even worse. And knowing the power he holds over these girls, it sounds so manipulative, almost like Olga didn't have a choice.

"She didn't listen to me, though," Monica continues. "Olga thought she was in love with Ryker, and was convinced he felt the same. She thought she'd change him. I mean, she didn't say that to me, but I could tell. That's why she started going kind of crazy."

"What do you mean by crazy?" I ask, even though I'm not sure I want to hear the answer.

"She wrote him letters, followed him, tried to talk to the other girls he spent time with, and even confronted him a couple of times."

"Confronted him?"

"Well, she tried to talk to him when he was with the posse. She tried to act like she was important to him."

"Wait, are you saying this is why she got kicked out?" I'm horrified.

"Well, there was also an incident with Winter Lovett," Ingrid says with resignation. "She walked in on Winter and Ryker in a storage room at the arena, and she kind of snapped. Olga and Winter were always rivals on the ice. They are the best. She did some stupid things, like messing with Winter's skates, and she tattled on her to the coaches about, well, stuff." Ingrid and Monica share a look.

"Guys?" I'm frustrated and sick of being out of the loop. "What stuff?"

"We're not supposed to talk about it," Monica says quietly.

"Just tell her. She's our friend. She won't talk about it."

"Winter was taking all these pills, illegal ones, for weight loss. She had a problem, and honestly, someone probably needed to tell the coaches. I'm pretty sure Winter's been getting help for it." Monica is defending Olga's "tattling," but Ingrid shakes her head.

"We don't tattle to faculty at Stark, Monica, you know that. It's a rule."

"There should be exceptions to the rule, when someone is in danger."

"Well, it became clear pretty quick that wasn't one of them," Ingrid almost snaps. And it dawns on me then that my friends' frustration and anger isn't directed at Ryker or his rules, but at Olga for breaking them. They respect Ryker. They respect his stupid rules. I'm speechless for the rest of the drive.

When we start our hike, and I'm following Ingrid and Monica, I ask the one question that's been nagging me the most. "So, all these girls, do they get with Ryker because they want to, or because they have to?"

Ingrid, who is in front, stops hiking and looks at me incredulously. "You've seen him, what do you think? I'd be down, even knowing what he's about, if he showed interest in me."

Monica doesn't answer.

"What if someone doesn't want to?" I ask.

Monica's head snaps up to mine. "You turned him down?" she gasps, awe written all over her face.

I shift uncomfortably. Why is that so unbelievable? "I'm sure I'm not the first. He's kind of a jerk."

"He's only going to chase you harder now," Ingrid says with a smirk. "Was that your plan?"

"No!" I shout, outraged.

"Relax, I get it. Well, some girls like knowing where they stand, and it makes things less complicated. For them, for him, for everyone. If you know up front that it's not going to be anything more than a hook-up, you don't have to waste your energy wondering." Ingrid begins hiking again and her words ring in my ears, reminding me of what Ryker said last night. It would be less complicated if he'd treated me like other girls.

"One more question. And this has to do with Monica and Liam more than anything." It's only a half-lie. "What are the rules about having real relationships at Stark? Do the rules with Ryker apply to everyone? I don't think I've seen any couples."

"We can date," Monica tells me. "But not many do. There's not much time, and it's not really a big thing."

"And the girls Ryker is with, they can date, too?"

Ingrid snorts. "The girls in the posse do whatever they want, if that's what you're asking. So do the guys. They don't care. And I don't think Ryker cares either, as long as no one's relationship becomes a problem."

Why does everything they say sound so cryptic? "Define problem." I feel like each word has a double meaning.

"For the Stark kingdom, of course," Ingrid says cheerily. "I told you your first day how Ryker's got his hand in all the important pots when it comes to winter sports."

"Yeah, yeah," I breathe out. My head is hurting from all this, and I can't bring myself to ask more questions about that piece of Ryker's life. He runs the school, I get that. Why exactly, I don't entirely understand, but I'll grill Ingrid and Monica about it later. I'm still reeling from their other disclosures about his personal life.

I can understand how an attractive guy like Ryker can get away with it though, because Brad isn't all that different. Somehow, the way Brad goes about his business seems less heartless. He doesn't act like women are meaningless to him. I mean, Chelsea and I are friends with him and he doesn't see us as conquests.

I'm reluctant to analyze my feelings about it, so I ask the girls what Liam and Misha are up to. Misha has borrowed Liam's car to go shopping at an outlet mall an hour and a half away, and Liam has a Skype date with his family, and is spending the rest of the day catching up on episodes of *The Walking Dead*.

"How was the rest of the dance?" I ask Monica.

"It was good," she says lightly. I'm still not sure if we're over our little argument, or if we're in deeper now that I know about Olga. But her tone returns to that song-like quality that tells me she's at ease as she describes dancing with Liam. "He kept dancing with me all night," she tells us. "One song after the next, and it wasn't anything like practice on the ice. We walked home together. With Misha too, but Liam gave me his jacket to wear."

"He's into you," I tell her.

"You think? I can't tell."

"He is, he just doesn't know what to do about it." I'm not entirely sure I know Liam well enough to make this kind of assessment, but I'm going with my gut instinct. Monica is adorable, caring, sweet, fun, and loyal. How could he not return her feelings?

We continue chatting about everything from the weather, which actually is a riveting issue for Ingrid and me, to the dance, to this pizza place the girls want to go for dinner tonight. Now that I know about Olga, and I understand Monica's reaction this morning, I think we're going to be fine.

After two hours' hiking, we hear laughter and voices. "Sounds like we'll be sharing the springs," Ingrid muses.

"That's weird, I didn't see any other cars in the lot," Monica says.

"Maybe they came in from the Stark property. The springs butt up against Stark land," Ingrid responds.

I assume she's talking about the mountain, but Monica grumbles, "It's probably the posse then. I bet they came from Ryker's house."

"Ryker's house?" I was there last night, and it wasn't on the ski mountain. It had a view of the mountain, but it was at least a mile away.

"Yeah, his house is the only one on the Stark property. You know he's a Stark, right?" Ingrid asks.

I choke out laughter. "A Stark?"

Both girls turn to look at me just before the trail peters out and we enter a clearing. "The Starks," Monica says slowly. "You know, the Stark family, who founded this town, built the resort, the academy..." She looks like she's going to continue adding on more accolades, but she stops short at my stunned expression.

"She didn't know," Monica says, looking at Ingrid now.

"You did not read the pamphlet about this place before you came, did you?" Ingrid scolds me.

"I read about the ski team, but I must have glossed over some parts," I admit. "We have our own heroes in Vermont. We don't pay attention to little ski towns out west," I argue, but I know this is information I should have been aware of from the beginning. It's one of many reasons Ryker Black didn't make sense to me, and the pieces of the puzzle are slowly falling into place.

"Girl, the Starks matter everywhere. Including Vermont," Ingrid states with finality.

Chapter 10

The voices in the hot springs quiet as we make our way over to a shed to change. I glance their way, recognizing each member of the posse, but none of them say hello. Ryker doesn't even make eye contact with me. After what he told me, more than once, and what the girls told me about Olga on the hike, this is entirely expected. Still, perhaps I'm just as naïve as Monica feared, and maybe I'm falling into the same trap as Olga did. Because I feel like maybe what we have is different. Didn't he say as much? He did bring me to his house; we didn't even kiss, except for that one on the forehead. Or was that a dream?

"Should we just go back?" Monica asks nervously. "They might kick us out."

"I want to go in. I say we go for it." We hiked all the way up here, didn't we?

It's freezing walking from the shed to the springs in our bathing suits, but the posse isn't blocking our entrance, and we climb into the hot water without confrontation. When I finally look up at the posse, I see they are all watching us.

"Hi, guys," I call over. Player and Cody have been friendly to me, and even Sven has warmed up a little, and they say hello with smiles, but as usual, I get the impression they are following Ryker's lead, and he's ignoring us.

He hops out, and it's then I notice several four-wheelers parked by a wide trail that's almost the size of a small road. My eyes follow Ryker as he walks over to one, as I'm sure everyone else's do. He opens the hatch on the back of one of the four-wheelers and pulls out a pony keg and a stack of plastic solo cups.

I think it's Telluride who whoops first when he starts to fill up cups, and then everyone in the posse is suddenly animated as they pass around the beer.

"What is that?" Monica whispers.

"A keg." And when I see her frown, I clarify. "Beer."

Ingrid and Monica share disapproving looks, and I have to agree. These people are supposed to be the best of the best, and my respect for them drops a notch as I watch them drink casually, as if they don't have the gifts of incredible talent and opportunity to waste.

Still, the sight of these elite athletes relaxing and enjoying themselves like normal teenagers is comforting. They aren't flawless training machines who never take a break. They stray from the perfect athletic regimen when temptation presents itself.

Ignoring the posse as they grow rowdier, the three of us settle into comfortable positions, lounging on the large rocks that provide underwater chairs and armrests, almost like a hot tub. The girls are telling me about the history of the springs, how it was discovered, and how most of it is totally natural, with only minimal additions like the rocks. I'm trying to listen but I can't ignore the sound of Winter flirting, and the low voice that occasionally responds.

Against my better judgment, I glance over, and it's not an image I want burned in my brain. Winter is sitting on Ryker's lap, facing him, so her legs are wrapped around his middle. Ryker is looking right at her, listening to whatever she's saying. Jealousy burns in my chest and I look quickly away, tilting my head back to rest on the rock and staring at the sky. Just yesterday, I hated Ryker. When did that change?

***

The snow blowing machines are out in full force through the month of October, and along with the rest of my teammates, I'm getting antsy. I'm stronger than I've ever been before, and I'm itching to feel the snow under my legs.

It's after a brutal agility session in the gym when Rocco announces we'll be hitting the snow tomorrow. "It's the earliest we've been out there in years, but there's a decent base layer at the top. Enough to set up slalom gates."

My teammates are buzzing at the news, and Ingrid is already talking about how we have to get to the mountain first thing so we can tune our skis before everyone else. "You know what? We should go tonight, after dinner, just to be safe," she says eagerly. She has more zeal for skiing than anyone I've ever met. Well, racing specifically.

"It's only going to take a few minutes, Ingrid." I try to calm her, but she's too excited.

Eventually, I relent to her enthusiasm and we borrow Liam's car after dinner to drive over to the mountain. The snow blowing machines are lit up and in high gear as they build up the giant mound of snow that will be made into the half pipe. Our key cards let us in the training hut, and we grab our skis from our lockers and bring them over to the work benches, where all the tools for waxing and sharpening are neatly organized.

The familiar process of getting skis ready for snow brings an onslaught of nostalgia and homesickness. At home, I usually tune my skis in my garage or at Brad's place, since it's close to the mountain and I often store my skis there.

Instead of classic rock, which is usually playing in Brad's garage, it's one of Ingrid's Euro hip-hop bands. But strangely enough, I feel at home here too, and with each passing day, I'm beginning to think I might just belong in this strange world. I just hope I'm able to hold my own on the slopes.

It doesn't take long for us to finish up, and Ingrid and I share excited glances at the snow-covered mountain as we make our way back to Liam's car. But his isn't the only one in the parking lot. A familiar pickup truck is beside it, and the driver's door opens as we approach.

"Ingrid, Roxanne," Ryker greets us with a nod.

"Hi Ryker," Ingrid says dutifully.

"I'll take Roxanne back to the dorms," he says without looking at me or asking. But I don't complain. I'm used to his rude behavior now. Since our overnight, this is the fourth time he's shown up unexpectedly, demanding to spend time with me. It's roughly a week apart, like he originally promised. And even though he's dismissive of Ingrid, I'm beginning to understand that he's not purposefully insulting her, and what's more, she doesn't take it that way. It's hard to grasp how someone like Ingrid would submit so easily to Ryker's abrasive ways, but she seems to accept that it's simply the order of things. People trust that Ryker is the way he is for a reason, and that he is, at the very least, a fairly equal-opportunity tyrant. No one, not even the posse, as far as I can tell, is immune from his wrath.

I still watch him carefully, and the way others react to him, trying to understand.

When Ingrid pulls away, Ryker approaches me, and leans against the hood of his truck.

"Were you getting your skis ready for tomorrow?"

"Yeah. You guys are going out too? The pipe isn't ready," I say, gesturing at the snow blowing machines.

"We'll do drills and jibs until more runs open up."

I nod. Of course, snowboarders have different events as well, but I've done my research, and I know that Ryker's best event is the half pipe.

"What are you doing out here?" I ask. He couldn't have known I'd be here, even if he did want to see me.

He smiles mischievously. "I like to be the first one to hit the snow at Stark Mountain every year. Want to join me?"

I answer without hesitation, "Hell, yes."

All my gear is in my locker and I pull it on eagerly, not even bothering to question how we're getting up there. Ryker's got a plan, I'm sure. Still, when I walk out of the training lodge and see the main lift moving, I'm a little startled. I guess I thought he had some sort of vehicle for getting up the mountain.

Ryker steps out of the lift operator's office, his frame outlined by the light behind him. So, he knows how to operate a ski lift. Is there anything he can't do?

"Not quite enough coverage for a snowmobile," he explains with a shrug before buckling into his board.

Riding on a lift for the first time each season is always a thrill. But as we glide forward into the night, with nothing but the sound of the snow blowers around us, it's like nothing I've ever experienced. Now that I know Ryker owns the mountain, I don't bother wondering how we're doing this, I just enjoy it. When it's only the two of us together, Ryker doesn't even pretend not to watch me. I've told him he has a staring problem, and he doesn't care. I know he's studying my reaction as I spin around and take in the lights of the academy and the town below.

"I've never been night skiing," I admit. "We don't have it at Sugarville."

"Officially, we don't have it at Stark either." Ryker is sitting close beside me, and it feels natural when I lean into him at the same time that he brings an arm around me. But this isn't anything like my comfortable friendship with Brad or Tyler. Even knowing Ryker's game with other girls, and letting him ignore me on campus, I still want to kiss him. Because when we're together, just the two of us, none of it matters. At least, I don't let it matter. He lets his guard down, and I know he doesn't do it with just anyone. I'll admit, I do feel special to him, though I try to tamp it down with the knowledge of Olga Popova. She thought she was special too. And it didn't end well.

We sit in comfortable silence on the way up, soaking in the eerie serenity. It's a stolen moment, one that I may never get again. I've never been on an empty ski lift or a mountain that won't open to the public for another three weeks.

We're at 13,000 feet when we reach the top of the second lift, but it's strangely calm. Ryker sits in the snow and I lean on my poles beside him, taking in the trail below. There's not much snow, but it's enough.

"I've never been up here at night without wind," Ryker comments. "It's perfect."

He's right. There's no swirling snow, fog or clouds blocking our view through the clear night air. I can see all the way to the bottom of the trail, where the first lift ends and the second lift begins.

I glance over at him and he gestures with his head to the trail below. "Ladies first."

I don't question it, even though I was waiting for him to slice the snow before me. I just go. And damn, it feels good. At first, I carve carefully, letting my legs remember how the skis feel. But as soon as I've got my momentum, I'm tucking in, pressing forward. The trail is barely lit by the lift, but I'm in full control as I arc one turn after the next. My muscles revel in the opportunity to work at what they love after months of preparation. I let out a cheer when I reach the bottom and throw my hands up in the air dramatically, like I've won a major race.

Ryker rides down the hill behind me, and he echoes my sentiment before joining me. "Again?" he asks, breathless, his eyes alight.

We keep at it for several runs, laughing and yelling ridiculously as we race each other to the bottom.

"This is, by far, the best first day back on skis I've ever had," I tell Ryker, when we eventually ride the first lift back to the bottom. There's not enough snow to ski all the way down. "Thank you."

He smiles and nods, but doesn't explain why he asked me to join him. Does he usually go by himself? Did he just happen to run into me tonight, and decided to go with it? There are so many questions I want to ask Ryker, and I just can't seem to do it. I'm afraid if I pry, it will break whatever spell has been cast.

Most of the times we've hung out have been at his house, in the giant loft. One time he caught me after practice, and we skipped class to go dirt biking. Still, he doesn't even look at me on campus. I've been trying not to over-analyze it, especially after all I've been told by him and by my friends, but it's not getting any easier.

Ryker makes a fire in the training hut while I take off my ski equipment. There are couches circled around a wood fireplace, which Ryker has burning bright, and with only one lamp on, I'd say this was a damn romantic ambience if I didn't know better.

I arrange some pillows on the floor so I can sit close by the fire, and Ryker settles in beside me. We watch the flames in silence for a few minutes, before I decide to ask one question that doesn't seem to have anything to do with us or the academy.

"Can you tell me about your mom?"

He goes very still beside me, and I take a cautious peek over at him. Ryker's staring straight ahead at the crackling fire.

"Why?" he whispers. It sounds like it hurts to get the word out.

"I want to understand you better," I respond simply. It's the truth.

"When people die, everyone talks about them like they were this amazing, wonderful person, even if they weren't. When someone dies unexpectedly, tragically, like my mom did, she's suddenly the world's greatest hero. I hated that. And I still do."

I don't say anything to that. I read about Elizabeth Stark, who kept her maiden name when she married, and I know that she died "suddenly and unexpectedly." The articles highlight her position as a leader for women in the business world. A tycoon in the ski industry who expanded her family's empire beyond alpine skiing, to all reaches of winter sporting activity. After reading about Stark, Inc. on Wikipedia, I was slightly appalled by my ignorance. The articles about Elizabeth briefly mentioned her surviving family members, but the main focus was on who would fill her shoes in the family business. Although, come to think of it, "family business" sounds friendly and homey, and "Stark empire" seems more fitting.

"She only wanted a kid so she could keep the legacy alive. There wasn't much maternal love in our house. And my dad was whipped. He thought she was perfect, and he fell apart when she died." Ryker isn't seeking sympathy, he's just reciting his life, and it happens to be a depressing one. In three sentences, he's unraveled a significant portion of the mystery that enshrouds him.

"Do you care about the legacy?"

He huffs out a chuckle and shakes his head. "You never say what I expect you to say, Roxanne. You never do what I expect, either. Each time I ask you to hang out, I wonder if you'll go off on me, or ignore me."

"Ask me? You never ask, Ryker, you just take."

He smirks, still staring at the fire. "That's only because I'm afraid you'll say no."

I purse my lips and elbow him in the ribs. "You're trying to distract me. Tell me about this Stark legacy that your mother cared so much about. It's all the businesses your family owns?"

His eyes snap away from the mesmerizing fire and turn to me, heated. "It's more than that. And I don't want to talk about it. You asked about my mother, and there's not much to say. She was strict, harsh, and, quite frankly, she frightened me."

Every once in a while, Ryker uses an expression like "quite frankly" and it makes him sound much older. But I'm not paying attention to that. The boy just told me he was afraid of his own mother. I'm not sure if I'm more shocked by the revelation itself, or that he shared it with me. I take his hand in mine, and lay off the questions for the rest of the night.

Chapter 11

"Hold up, go over this one more time," Chelsea says. "You went *skiing* last night, when the mountain was closed?"

"Well, it opens for Stark today, but yeah, I'm telling you, Ryker Black, like, owns the mountain or something. He can do whatever he wants."

Chelsea has to know every detail, and when I tell her that I fell asleep on his chest in front of the fire, she gets really fired up. "Roxie, you can't tell me that Ryker Black isn't totally into you." She always refers to him by his full name, like he's a celebrity.

"Well then, explain why he pretends he doesn't know me the rest of the time, and why he hasn't made a move."

Chelsea's at a loss on that one. "It's weird. I'll give you that. But you said he's a totally different guy when he's with you. Maybe all this ruling the school bullshit means he has to act all tough and scary on campus."

"He can be a real asshole," I confirm. There's no one else I feel I can talk to about Ryker. It seems like I'd be breaking a rule, or at least betraying his confidence somehow, if I dissected his behavior and attitude with anyone at Stark. Not to mention that my friends have a biased opinion based on what happened with Olga Popova. I should talk to Brad about it, because he does have the whole non-commitment thing in common with Ryker, but Brad would just get all protective on me.

"You really need to figure out why he has so much control over everything at the academy," Chelsea speaks in a hushed voice, as if Ryker can hear her in Vermont. "It sounds like there's something going on, don't you think?"

"You think it's more than the family name and his inheritance of basically the entire school and the mountain, too? Do you really think he makes the big decisions about stuff? I mean, the guy is snowboarding at international competitions. It's not like he's actually involved with the businesses he apparently owns."

"He doesn't really own them, Roxie," Chelsea says, and I can practically hear her rolling her eyes. "He just inherited shares or money or something. The guy hasn't even graduated high school."

"But he knows how to operate a ski lift," I remind her.

"Clearly he's capable of running the world, then."

"Later dude, time for me to go skiing." I love rubbing it in her face.

"My green-eyed monster will be hiding under your bed tonight."

When we get to the top of the mountain that morning, Lia and Rocco are already setting up slalom gates. We get one warm-up run, and then we inspect the course, which means we slowly slide through the gates, noting how they are lined up, and making a strategic plan on how to run them. After that, we do six runs on the course, which is about the max before it becomes super rutted and our legs are shot.

I'm into it for about three runs, but I've never liked slalom. Slalom is when the gates are really close together, one right after the next, and they're flexible so you can hit them with your pole or shins and they bend out of your way so that you don't have to go all the way around the gate and slow down your line. It's the most technical discipline, with GS, or giant slalom, also falling into the tech category, though the gates are a little farther apart in GS.

Most skiers start to specialize in tech or speed around my age, but it was clear years ago for me. I'm a speed racer. The super-G, which has the gates even farther apart, was always my best discipline, until I got to try the downhill, which has hardly any gates and is basically straight down the mountain as fast as you can go. Downhill is super dangerous and requires three days of course inspections and practice runs before we're allowed to race.

Anyway, it's slalom today, since there's not enough terrain to run GS or super-G, which are much longer courses. And even though

I'm pumped to be on snow, it's all about perfect technique and control, which just isn't my thing. I want to be able to feel the curve of each turn and the wind whipping by me as I pick up speed. There are just so many gates to get through with slalom that it's impossible to think about anything else.

There's also the fact that Lia is all over me, pointing out every little detail on what I can change or improve. It's only the first day on skis, and she's hounding me about my posture, my rhythm, my arm position. It's not nearly as much fun as last night.

By the time practice wraps up, I'm feeling pretty bummed that my first training session on snow was a letdown. Each time I tried to fix whatever Lia mentioned, she'd have something new to work on. It's not that I don't like to work on technique, but there's only so much fine-tuning I can take in one session. I've always been more about the speed. If I can't rip my way down a trail, and there are gates blocking my momentum every second, I get a little frustrated.

Ingrid, on the other hand, is practically floating. Slalom is her best event, and she was totally in her element today. She hardly seems to notice my own mood when we go to DH after practice. I try to shake it off, knowing we won't be doing slalom gates every day, and it was only my first practice on skis at Stark, but my sour mood sticks with me. I'm sure it doesn't help that Ryker ignores me, once again, and Petra makes a passing comment implying that I'm not Stark caliber.

The figure skaters have a team function, and it's lonely in my dorm room. I've got a little homework I could do, but my mind is determined to remain in moping mode and it doesn't want a distraction. Sometimes a girl just needs a little time to wallow in self-pity.

Lying back on my bed, I consider calling my parents or my friends as I typically do this time of night, but I don't really want to talk about it. I don't want to tell them that my first practice on snow at Stark was a major fail. They'd tell me that it was slalom, which I've never really liked, and that I'm only going to improve. I try to encourage myself with the words that Brad, Chelsea, Tyler or Mom and Dad would say, but it doesn't really help. After intense dryland training for the past two months, I really had high hopes I'd start out on the snow with a bang. I've been imagining it every night when I fall asleep, that I'd finally prove myself to my teammates. I know they are skeptical that I've got what it takes to be here, Petra especially, and today I didn't exactly change their opinions.

Even Ingrid, who's always been on my side, seems to think of me as a little bit of a charity case. My confidence is really taking a hit going from the top of the food chain at Sugarville to the bottom at Stark.

My eyes snap open when I hear a knock and before I can even swing my legs around to hop up, the door opens. He looks around the room, assessing my side with greater attention before taking a seat on my bed, without invitation. Ryker hasn't been in here since that very first day, and his presence tonight is both thrilling and unwelcome. But then, without a word, he unloads a grocery bag, and my attitude changes.

"I wasn't sure what flavor you liked, so I got a few choices."

When he's done unpacking the bag, six different flavors of Ben and Jerry's ice cream are laid out before me.

"You got six pints of ice cream? Is there a party going on I don't know about?"

"You looked upset at DH," Ryker says hesitantly. "Don't girls eat ice cream when they're upset?"

The tentativeness in his voice is adorable. So much so, that I have to refrain from leaning forward and kissing him. Not a passionate one, just a "damn you're sweet" peck, like a girlfriend might give. I lean back instead, suddenly nervous I may do something I'll regret.

"Why are you being so nice? Did I really look that pathetic?"

Ryker chuckles. "You're pretty hard on yourself, aren't you? It was just the first practice, Roxanne, and slalom's not your thing." He says just what my parents or Brad might say, and it makes me frown. What kind of relationship do Ryker and I have, anyway?

It dawns on me, then, why he might be here. "Did Petra say something to you?" I look up at him, and he takes off his beanie before answering.

"Petra feels threatened by you, Roxanne. She's going to cut you down however she can. She might be the team captain, but she's not on your side."

My hand stills halfway to the Cherry Garcia at Ryker's ominous warning. "What does she have against me?" And why would I be a threat to someone like Petra Hoffman?

Ryker watches me open the Cherry Garcia. "Is that your favorite?"

"Yes."

He looks quite pleased with himself for choosing it. "I've never had it."

"I'm surprised you found it out here. Where do they sell Ben and Jerry's in Stark, by the way? It's a Vermont company."

"I know. That's why I got it. The grocery sells it. Have you been to the one in town yet?"

"No, I always go to DH."

"You've been to Mario's," Ryker states.

My eyes narrow before I take my first bite. "How do you know that?"

Ryker smirks. "I know everything."

"Then answer my question. What's Petra's deal? Why does she hate me?"

"I told you. You're a threat."

I savor the ice cream for a moment before scolding Ryker. "For someone who knows everything, that's not a valid reason. Her FIS points are way lower than mine, and she's probably going to make the German team next year." Race points are like dominos – the low score wins.

"It's not just about that," Ryker says, leaning back against the wall so he's sitting horizontally across the bed, his feet hanging off the edge. He kicks off his shoes, and now I've got Ryker Black, barefoot, lounging in my bed. "Petra's set herself up to be the next big thing in women's ski racing, or women's sports in general. She's got the talent, the looks, and the connections to do it. You have the first two, and now you're at Stark, which means you might just get the connections too. She's watching closely."

"That's stupid," I say dismissively, and Ryker's lips twitch, like he may laugh. "Ingrid's the only one on the team who's beaten Petra. If there's anyone Petra should feel threatened by, it's Ingrid."

Ryker studies me for a long moment, his arms crossed. "Do you want me to point out the obvious, Roxanne?"

"I think I'm the one pointing out the obvious here, Ryker. Ingrid's going to make the Austrian National Team, and plenty of girls at Stark have what it takes to be the next big thing in skiing. Isn't that why we're all here?"

"Yes. Everyone has potential to make it big. But Petra wants to be the biggest, the best, the most well-known. She wants the fame, the money, the prestige, the power. She wants it all. Ingrid Koller just wants to win on the slope. She's got a good head on her shoulders for competition, and she's presentable, but not stunning. Her family is well connected in Austria's alpine industry, but it's not far-reaching like the Hoffmans."

He reaches and pulls the spoon right out of my hand before I can take my next bite, and puts it into his own mouth.

"People aren't that shallow, Ryker. You don't have to be gorgeous to be a popular athlete. And you don't need to know the CEO of a company to get them to sponsor you." I mean, I'd been sponsored for years, along with many of my triple-S teammates back in Vermont, and even though those sponsorships were just for our equipment, small potatoes in the scheme of things, it's not like we had "connections."

"Maybe not, but if you want to be a household name, someone who goes down in history, you need it all."

It's a pointless conversation, as far as I'm concerned. I'm not sure what my long term goals are for skiing, but I've never considered myself in the same league as Petra Hoffman. There must be a different reason for Petra's animosity towards me. At least Ryker didn't try to deny it. She probably trash-talks me. I'm curious what she says, and if Ryker tries to defend me. Are we even friends? Why is he here?

"You know," I tell him, passing another bite of ice cream, "I've been meaning to ask you an important question."

"What's that?"

"Did you bug our room?"

He grins. "Is that what your roommate told you?"

I shrug, not wanting to throw Monica under the bus, but needing an answer.

"No," he answers. "But I would if I thought I needed to. I've never had to bug a room before," he reflects, as though it's something he totally might do at some point.

If I was going to get Ryker's side of the story about Olga Popova, now would be a good time to do it. But I'm not sure I want to know. I'm not sure I'll ever want to know everything about Ryker. Maybe I'm still in denial, because otherwise, I doubt I'd be sitting in my dorm room eating ice cream with him.

"What about you? Are you trying to be the next big thing in snowboarding?" It feels like a silly question. Ryker can do whatever he wants, can't he?

But his expression darkens at that question, and he doesn't respond. Instead, he checks his cell phone, even though he'd been ignoring its vibrations earlier.

"Want to go sledding?" he asks, typing something on his phone.

"Right now?" I glance out the window. It's dark.

"Yeah. Should be nice and slick since there's not much snow yet."

"Uh, sure." Why not?

Ryker's already sliding off the bed. "Want me to put the ice cream in the fridge?" he asks.

"Nah, no freezer, it'll melt. There's one downstairs."

"We'll just bring it. The guys can eat it."

"The guys?"

"Player, Cody, Sven. We're meeting them. Grab a coat."

He's bringing me to hang out with the posse? This is new.

I want to ask if Petra will be there, but I don't want Ryker to think I'm afraid of her. I'm not. I just want to be prepared.

Ryker pulls up in front of one of the guys' dorms, and I'm unsure whether I should let one of his friends ride shotgun, until I hear shouts and a banging on the back of the pickup. Looking out the rear window, I see the three boys, with sleds, have already piled into the bed of the truck.

Ryker turns up the radio and hits the gas, so the guys go sprawling behind us. He smiles, the guys yell, and strangely, I feel like I belong here.

Chapter 12

The guys almost treat me like one of them. There's no flirting, no weirdness about a girl being with them. They act like it's totally normal for Ryker to bring along a random girl they hardly know. It almost makes me wonder if he does this often. Maybe Ingrid and Monica don't know everything about how he operates, after all.

Ryker drives us to a hill behind the post office in town, and there's no one else around, even though the snow is packed down with tracks from other sledders. It quickly turns into a competition, and although I weigh less than the guys, I've got excellent technique when it comes to a running start, and I'm able to hold my own.

"It's your sled, Roxie, you waxed it before we left, didn't you?" Player's a sore loser. Seriously, who waxes a sled as if it's a ski or snowboard?

"You brought the sleds, Player, remember?"

"Did you sabotage mine?" He holds his up, looking for holes. "I've got like, at least forty pounds on you. The law of gravity says I should win."

"Maybe you're too heavy for your sled. It probably has a weight limit."

"Let's switch sleds and do a rematch," he argues.

I beat him again, and he decides to console himself with chocolate fudge brownie ice cream in the back of the pickup. It's only twenty degrees out, but the other guys join him, each eating an entire pint on his own. It's impressive.

"You head out tomorrow, right man?" Cody asks. He's looking at Ryker, who's leaning against the back of the truck, and Ryker looks at me.

I'm sitting on the edge, at the opposite side from him, but even through the dark, his aqua eyes are mesmerizing. He turns them to

Cody. "First thing in the morning. It will be two, maybe three weeks."

The guys nod, and the mood changes from playful and lighthearted to serious. I want to ask where he's going, but something tells me I should wait until we're alone. "New York first, right? Then Paris and London?" Sven asks.

Ryker nods, and the guys fire questions about who will be there, which companies he's interested in, who's got the best marketing strategy, the best contracts with athletes this season, and whether he plans on hanging out with certain individuals, some names I recognize as Stark graduates, others I've never heard before. From what I gather, Ryker is making the rounds as a rep of some sort for Stark, though I'm not sure if it's for his family business or for the academy, or both. I suppose he is a good representative, if the point is to bring a good image. He's got the three qualities he mentioned earlier – looks, talent, and connections. He and Petra could take over the world together. Maybe she's even accompanying him on this trip. And just like that, I've distanced myself again, which is probably for the best. I don't even know what they're talking about; I'm just an outsider, here at Stark for the ride, but not really part of their world.

As if he can sense my shift in mood, Ryker announces that we're heading back, and the guys don't argue. He jumps out the side of the bed, and takes my hand to help me out, even though I don't need it. He even loads me into the passenger seat, his sudden attentiveness a bit disarming. Maybe Ryker Black is all-knowing after all, and if he is, why is he so determined to put me at ease?

He doesn't say anything on the way back to campus, and I assume he's waiting to drop off the guys before he explains his trip to me. But he pulls up to my dorm first, and I realize I won't be getting any explanation at all.

"I'll see you in a couple weeks, Roxanne." I don't know why this is such a big deal to me, since we usually only see each other once a week, on his terms, but I'm really upset. Unreasonably disappointed. Mostly, I'm confused. He acts so sweet one minute, and totally dismissive the next.

"Yeah, see you later." I think I do a decent job of echoing his indifferent tone, but inside I'm reeling.

"If you need anything, just let the guys know," he tells me before I can climb out. I sense that those words are weighty ones. He's given me a "connection" or a stamp of approval in his world. Whatever it is, I'd rather have something different from him, though I'm not sure he's capable of what I want.

I force a smile and a wave to the guys in the back before turning to head into my dorm.

I'm about to take the stairs when Winter and Aspen come out of the common area, looking pissed.

"Why did Ryker just drop you off?" Aspen asks, hands on hips. The girl is always dressed for a hipster fashion shoot, and tonight is no exception.

"Where did you guys go? Why were you with them?" Winter goes for more of a preppy look, and she's got on one of her signature argyle sweaters with moccasin-style boots that actually look very comfortable, if not all that functional in the snow.

Neither of them are shouting, and their voices are actually soft and controlled, but I know there's a bite behind them. Those are *their* guys, and they don't appreciate any intruders. If I didn't know I was one before, I do now.

"They saw me downtown and gave me a ride." The lie comes easily, and I don't even consider telling them the truth. For some reason, it seems like the truth, as innocent as it was, could be dangerous for me. Joining the posse guys for something as low-key as sledding and ice cream is a big deal at Stark. And my instincts tell me I should keep it a secret.

Winter and Aspen exchange a look. They don't believe me. Aspen asks, "Why would they do that? Those guys don't go around offering random girls rides."

I shrug. "Are you my keeper? Or theirs? I don't think so."

Aspen's eyes narrow and she takes a step forward. Winter places a hand on her arm. "Which one are you hooking up with, Roxie?" Winter asks, a false sweetness permeating her question.

Ignoring them, I continue up the stairs. Let them draw their own conclusions. But then I hear footsteps come up behind me and my ponytail is yanked back, hard. I'm so shocked, I yelp. A moment later, a few doors open, and now I know we've got an audience.

I spin around, ready to push off whoever's got my hair, but I'm slammed against the wall, and the two girls have me pinned. Aspen's face is inches from mine when she speaks. "Stay away from the posse, Roxie. If they want to hook up with you, fine, but you won't take rides from them, and you will never be their friend. Got it?"

Winter releases my ponytail then and the girls go back downstairs and into the common room. I'm too shaken to respond. Part of me wants to follow them and take them on, tell them they've got no right to dictate my friendships, but part of me just doesn't care enough. It all seems so silly and tiresome. Why do they even care? What's the big deal? And besides, I'm not sure I even have any friendships with their guys worth fighting for.

The door to our dorm room is open, and Monica is sitting on the edge of her bed. She must have heard what went down.

Closing the door behind us, I start with good news. "Well, Ryker didn't bug our room, so we can talk freely now."

She gives me a tight smile. "Do you know what you're doing, Roxie?"

"Nope." Flopping onto my bed, I grumble into my pillow, "Why can't people here be normal?"

Monica comes over to sit on the floor beside me. "Stark is not normal, Roxie. You've figured that out by now, haven't you?"

"If I didn't already know it, then that little episode in the stairwell definitely sent the message."

"The posse girls wanted Olga out too, you know. They didn't like her hanging around Ryker so much, and as soon as she made a wrong move against Winter, she sealed her fate."

"Sometimes I just want to go back home, where I don't have to watch my back all the time, worried I'll make a misstep."

"If only Ryker hadn't shown an interest in you, you'd be fine."

"He's leaving for a couple weeks. Maybe he'll forget about me when he gets back."

Monica doesn't look so certain. "You really aren't hooking up with him, are you?"

I shake my head. "He's so confusing."

"Yeah," Monica agrees. "Hey, how was your first time on snow?" Monica asks, suddenly remembering that today was the big day.

"Not great," I admit. "We did slalom gates for two hours straight, and Lia hammered me on my technique. She pretty much called me out in front of the entire team for being totally inept at slalom."

"Wow. That sucks."

"Yeah. I'm pretty depressed about it," I say, but I'm not feeling so mopey now. I've actually got some fighting spirit back, especially after getting harassed by Winter and Aspen. I'm determined to prove that I belong here, if not with the posse, than at least on the Stark alpine team.

"I hear that Lia can be kind of a bitch, but she knows what she's doing."

"Is that what Ingrid says?"

"That's what everyone says. She wouldn't bother hammering you if she didn't think you'd respond and get better. Ingrid used to have a hard time with her a couple of years ago, but then she started improving. Just hang in there and don't let her beat you down. The coaches here don't exactly take the nice approach. You've got to be able to handle the criticism."

"Your coaches are tough, too?"

"They still make me cry sometimes," she admits. "I usually call my mom and she makes me feel better. Olga never had much sympathy for it. I guess the coaches at Stark were nothing compared to her coaches in Russia."

Before going to bed later that night, I check my phone and see a message from a Colorado cell phone number.

This is Ryker if you need to reach me.

Does he want me to call him while he's away, or only in case I "need" to reach him? It should weird me out that he got my cell phone number without my knowledge, but it doesn't surprise me. Would he want to know what his friends said to me? Probably not. One moment, it seems he cares about me and the next I feel disposable, like maybe I'm a project.

***

"What are you so afraid of?" Lia Moretti asks me, for the third time this morning.

"I'm not. I'm trying to do what you say, I'm just not good at slalom." I keep telling her this, and she won't accept it. It's been three weeks of slalom, and nothing else. Maybe once she sees me on super-G she'll chill out. The woman is relentless.

"No, you say that. But you just don't want to be good at slalom. You fight it. You can't fight it when the gates come so fast. You have to embrace them, and find a rhythm with them." It's the first time she's used flowy language like this. She usually just shouts at me to move my body a particular way. I wonder if she's giving up. For some reason, her rich Italian accent makes each syllable out of her mouth more powerful.

"Stop waiting for super-G and downhill," she says, as if she can read my mind. "Get better here, on slalom." She gestures to the course below. "And then you will improve everywhere. You are holding back. You are content to be so-so," she says, moving her gloved hand back and forth. It's the first time, ever, a coach has told me I'm only average. By Stark standards, she's right. And I really don't like to hear it. "You don't believe you can be better? You don't want it? You are afraid to be the best? Figure it out." And then, like she always does after critiquing my form, she nods that it's time for me to do the run. I'm beginning to think everyone at Stark is nuts.

I run the course angrily this time, letting the gates snap harshly as I cross-block them, swiveling through the deep tracks we've created from hours of skiing. I'm not thinking about Lia's endless pointers, just her taunts that I'm content being average. I'll show her average. I'm burning through this course with a fierceness that makes me feel invincible.

When I get to the bottom, I'm panting harder than usual, and Lia lets out a loud whoop from the top of the course. Apparently that was the response she was looking for. But I'm done for the day, whether or not practice is officially over. The trail to the bottom recently opened, and I need to do some real skiing. The last time I did turns without the watchful eyes of the coaches was that night with Ryker.

Instead of stopping at the mid-way lift, I keep going, picking up speed as the slope dips. The wind whips past my cheeks, and I revel in the feeling of pure speed, with no gates or tracks inhibiting my momentum. I'm in a racing tuck now, as aerodynamic as possible as I carve my way down to the bottom, my heart racing with adrenaline.

I'm not expecting to see anyone when I reach the training hut. I've ditched the workout, and everyone is still at the top of the mountain. The snowboarders must be arriving though, because I make out a rider walking toward me, his board tucked under his arm.

It's been three weeks since I've seen or heard anything from Ryker, and here he is, ready to ride and looking devastating as usual. Whether it's a combination of the rush of the run with Lia's comments, or the sudden appearance of this boy, I have the strange urge to burst into tears. Afraid I'll lose it in front of him, I keep my momentum and ski right past Ryker, quickly snapping out of my bindings before he can catch me.

The lodge is empty, with my teammates still on the mountain and, apparently, Ryker the only rider around at the moment. But just as I slide out of my ski boots, the air shifts around me, and I know he's followed me.

"Roxanne." His voice is gruff and holds a weightiness to it that I can't decipher the meaning of.

I glance over to him, leaning against a locker with his arms crossed, watching me.

"Hi, Ryker." What does he want from me? I slip off my snowpants, hang them in my locker, and pull on Uggs over my long underwear. "Back from your trip?"

"I got in this morning," he tells me.

When I look up, he's moved closer, so he's only a foot away from me. I'm tired of Ryker playing around with me like this, hot and cold, into me one minute and ignoring me the next. I'm sick of Lia hounding me, trying to play with my head, find the deeper meaning for why I don't click on the slalom gates. I just want to ski, dammit. I came here to ski, and it's only when there's no one around, when I'm rushing down that hill like I did just now, that I can enjoy myself.

And now Ryker's even ruined the rush from that, cutting it short by showing up and throwing around my emotions like a toy. I missed him, but I shouldn't have. I want to hug him, kiss him, jump in his arms, but I should really be running the other way.

"Why are you so upset?" he asks.

I just shake my head, afraid if I open my mouth, I'll be a rambling disaster.

But then he cups my cheek with his hand and rubs a thumb lightly along my cheekbone, and I'm already crumbling.

"Tell me, Roxanne. I just got back, and I had heard everything was fine. And then I see you like this, and I'm wondering what I missed."

"Everything was fine? Who told you that? Petra? Never mind. Things *are* fine, Ryker. I just suck at slalom and that's all we've been doing for the past three weeks. It's getting to me."

Ryker's eyes narrow. "That's all?"

I close my eyes, and for some reason, I feel like Ryker's the only person who might understand if I tell him what Lia said. "Lia's been at me about technique every day, but just now, she got on me about something else, and I didn't like it."

Ryker's eyes hold mine, searching, listening.

"She asked me what I was afraid of, and told me that I just don't want to be good at slalom, that I'm content to be so-so." I mimic Lia's hand movements. "It was like she was mocking me. Of course I want to be the best I can be. That's why I'm here."

Ryker watches me for a long moment. "Maybe it stung because there's some truth to what she's saying."

I open my mouth to protest but his fingers on my lips stop me.

"Lia is one of the best slalom coaches in the world, Roxanne. Don't write her off. She wasn't trying to insult you for no particular reason. She was trying to figure out why, after three weeks, she hasn't seen the results from you she wants or expects. And if she has high expectations for you, you should be flattered. Lia doesn't get so worked up about everyone, I'm sure you've noticed. She thinks you can be a lot better than you already are, and wants you to get there."

A brick on my chest slides away slowly as he speaks. His voice is low and soothing, and he seems to understand so much more about the situation than I do. It makes me want to contemplate Lia's words and put my emotions aside to do some introspection. Maybe there is some truth to it, and if anyone else had told me that, I'd be even angrier. But when Ryker pauses in his world domination mission to say something to me about my skiing, I want to listen.

A sound of disgust sends me a step away from Ryker. Petra has entered the locker room and she looks between us in outrage. "Nice pep talk, Ryker." The sarcasm is heavy, and I've never heard anyone, except maybe myself, speak to Ryker this way. "Why don't you tell her to toughen up or get out, like you do everyone else who can't handle a little criticism?"

Ryker takes a heavy step toward her. "You have a problem with the way I'm speaking to Roxanne?"

"Hell yes I do. She's been moping around ever since we got on skis and she realized she's not the queen of the mountain like she is in Vermont. It's about time she got a backbone and listened to what the coaches are telling her, not cry about it. She's no one special, Ryker, so stop treating her like it. It's a waste of your time. Of everyone's time."

I'm about to defend myself, but I have no words. There's some truth to what Petra's saying, and I hate that.

Ryker tilts his head to the side. "Don't question me on how I speak to Roxanne. Not everyone comes from your background, Petra. Not everyone is born with an understanding of the way things work at Stark. We're not going to scare her off when the season's barely started. She's got what it takes. Lia knows it. Rocco knows it. I know it. And you know it. So stop trying to get me to push her to the breaking point. You know we don't do that with everyone. She's not one of the weak ones. She's not a mistake."

Petra makes another snort of disgust and brushes past him with a nasty glare in my direction.

I don't know what to say when Ryker turns around to face me. He just defended me in the strangest way. And what if I don't prove him right? What if I am "one of the weak ones?" What does that even mean?

He steps closer to me and speaks quietly. "I want to see you tonight. I'll pick you up outside your dorm at eight. Be waiting."

All I can do is nod.

Chapter 13

Something is different about Ryker tonight. We're sitting on the couch in his loft, listening to music, and I've never seen him so still. He's got something on his mind, and I want to know what it is.

"Are you going to tell me about your trip?"

He turns from staring out the window, and runs a hand through his light curls. "I wasn't planning on it, no."

"Why am I here, Ryker?"

His eyes flash dark for a second. "What do you mean?"

"I think you know exactly what I mean."

"You're here because I want you here, Roxanne."

I push his chest at that. I'm not putting up with his evasive non-answers. "That's not good enough. Why do you open up to me about some things and close me out about others? Why are you nice to me sometimes and ignore me others? Why would you want to hang out with me, like a friend? *Are* we friends? I just don't get it."

"I'm not going to give you answers to those questions, Roxanne, so drop it."

"No."

"No?" His eyes narrow at the challenge.

"I'm not going to drop it. Are we friends?"

"Sure. We're friends, Roxanne." He's humoring me and there's no seriousness about his response.

"Fine, then tell me about your trip. Friends would explain why they disappeared for three weeks."

"You heard the guys talking the night before I left. You know enough."

"Enough to know I'm in the dark."

Ryker shifts forward on the couch, and my heart rate picks up. "You can be very difficult, Roxanne Slade, you know that?"

He's gone from contemplative, to argumentative, to flirtatious in the span of minutes. At least I *think* this is Ryker flirting, but I can't be sure.

"You like it," I say, swallowing nervously as he leans closer.

"I don't know why, but you're right."

His lips are inches from mine now.

"Are you going to kiss me, or are you teasing me?" I ask because I need to know, right this instant. I want him to kiss me, and if he's not going to, then he needs to stop acting like he will before I do something really stupid.

His lips are practically touching mine when he asks, "Do you want me to kiss you?"

"Yes," I respond without hesitation.

It's slow and delicate when his lips meet mine. He takes his time, in no rush to go anywhere. He's nothing like the other two boys I've kissed. Ryker is deliberate with each soft caress, each movement. His hands know just where to touch on my neck and face, and he doesn't even try to lower them. It only makes me ache for that, and I try to shift my hips to encourage him, but he steadies me with his own strength. We're pressed close, and I let my arms drift to the hair I've been wanting to run my hands through since the very first time we met. It's as soft as I imagined, and my fingers clutch onto the curls by his neck as he tugs my body to his until I'm straddling his lap.

It's then that the unwelcome image of Winter and Ryker at the hot springs assaults me, and my body freezes in Ryker's arms. He's dazed when I pull away.

This is what I wanted, but I don't want to be just another girl to Ryker. I can't do it if that's all this is. No matter how nice his kisses feel, and his body underneath mine feels amazing, I know I'll feel horrible about myself if I let it go any further than this. If we keep doing this, I need him to feel more for me, like I do him. Whether I wanted it or not, Ryker Black has a hold on me, and I won't surrender anything more unless he's willing to do the same.

"Roxanne?" He's confused, and I can't blame him.

"I think I should go home now."

"But you just got here."

"I'm not going to kiss you anymore, Ryker, if you're going to be doing this with other girls."

I'm still sitting on his lap, and when I shift back, he hisses out a breath.

"So, you're just teasing me, then?" He's angry, and that makes me angry.

"Yeah, maybe I am." I'll admit it, I said that I wanted him to kiss me and pulled away as soon as it got heated. I should have had this conversation with him beforehand, but here we are.

"I want to kiss you again, Roxanne, but I'm not going to make any promises."

I shrug, like it doesn't make a difference to me, even though his words hurt. It's not like he didn't warn me from the first time I came over, and my friends didn't tell me how it is. But I still hoped it'd be different for me. "Fine. We'll go back to just friends, then."

Sliding off his lap leaves me cold, and Ryker doesn't seem all that inclined to let me go. His grip remains firm until I put some distance between us and his hands slip away. We watch each other from opposite ends of the coach.

"You are so difficult," he growls.

"So are you," I point out.

"I'm never going to be your boyfriend, Roxanne, if that's what you want." His voice drips with condescension. "I don't do the boyfriend thing."

"I noticed."

"Is that what you want? A boyfriend?"

I shake my head. Is that what I was saying? I don't want him to be with anyone else if we keep doing this. And I don't want it to be a one-time thing. And I want him to feel something for me, though I can't force that. All those things signify boyfriend, yet I don't think that's really what I want. This is stupid.

"I've never even had a boyfriend, Ryker. I just don't want you to be kissing lots of other girls if you're going to be kissing me." That's easy enough, right?

He shakes his head, opens his mouth to say something and then closes it.

"What?" I want to know what he was going to say.

"You've never had a boyfriend? Seriously?"

"Have you ever had a girlfriend?" I counter. I'm pretty sure I already know the answer.

"No. I just... really? You've never had a boyfriend?"

"No, Ryker, I have never had a boyfriend."

He contemplates this for at least a full minute. "Have you demanded this exclusivity from other guys, then?"

I cross my arms and narrow my eyes. Nosy. He's going to find out just how inexperienced I am if he keeps prying, and then he'll think my "demand" has less credibility. "I never had to. It was implied." I'm talking about Colton Lennox, and that whole thing only lasted a month this summer.

"And it's not implied here, since you actually told me it's never that way with you." And everyone else on campus seems to know it, too,

I want to add. I'd go on, mentioning how he ignores me outside of our meetings, but I don't have the energy, and don't really see a point. He does things the way he wants, and if we're going to do more than hang out together, he's going to have to make at least this one concession.

"Let's watch a movie," he declares. I don't resist. A movie actually sounds nice, since then we don't have to talk about what just happened, or didn't happen. And I'm not ready to go home yet. What if this is our last time together?

But this time, we don't naturally lean in towards each other when we watch the movie. Instead, we make a conscious effort to keep some space between us. Or at least, I do. I can't tell what Ryker is thinking. He doesn't seem to care one way or the other, and that pisses me off. Actually, it hurts like hell, but I try to channel it into anger.

I find that channeling anger helps at practice the next day, too. I never asked what being "one of the weak ones" meant, but I'm determined to prove that I'm not it. Petra thinks I should get scared off with tough love, that I can't handle it here, and I'm not going to let her be right.

Lia doesn't say anything to me on the warm-up run, doesn't even comment on me ditching the end of practice yesterday. A new course is set up, and I consciously shift attitudes as I eye it on the way up the lift. I'm going to burn through it today like I'm making a point. I'm going to own the course as if I really could be good at slalom.

"What do you think about when you're doing gates?" I ask Ingrid, who's riding up beside me.

"Huh? I don't know. Is there even time to think? All my thinking about the course is beforehand. Once I'm running it, I just go as fast as I can."

"Even training? Like, what about when Lia tells you to fix or change something? Aren't you trying to do it?"

"Oh, yeah, I guess so. But only like, in the back of my mind. I get all tense when I overthink. That's why I'm not as good at super-G and downhill. The gates don't come fast enough so there's too much time to think."

I laugh at that. "We're opposites then. I like the rush of going fast without so many gates. I overthink everything when I'm doing slalom."

"Yeah, you do." Ingrid doesn't sugarcoat it. "I can practically hear you thinking when you're training. I assumed you were always like that when you skied."

"I'm going to try not to overthink it today."

"Yeah." Ingrid fist-bumps me. "Slalom actually feels fast if you don't think about it much."

"Right." I'm being sarcastic, but when I try it out, I see what Ingrid is saying. The gates become a blur and the quick turns take on a fluid motion, almost like dancing.

Lia's quietness doesn't last. I hear her call out, "Roxie!" just as I hit the last gate.

I glance up the hill and she shouts down from partway up the course. "Better. Now just attack it with some aggression like yesterday."

I nod. It's the first time she's said anything encouraging to me. Apparently I respond better to emotional coaching rather than technical. All I really need to do to get aggressive is think about beating Petra. Sure, it's a long shot, but it gets my blood pumping. Lia wolf-whistles when I finish the next run, and Ingrid does the same. And the rest of the practice goes similarly. Even Sven lets out some whoops. As the course gets more rutted, and more difficult to ski, I become even more determined to keep it up. By the time Rocco calls it quits for the day – he's the more passive coach for slalom training – my legs are toast, but I know I've had a breakthrough.

Everyone is chattering about the storm coming in tonight on the shuttle ride back to campus. It means that the rest of the mountain will be opening soon. The official opening day is tomorrow, the Saturday before Thanksgiving. The storm is just in time. The amount of snow we have accumulated already is unusual, and they're predicting over a foot in this storm.

"You were a rock star out there today, Roxie." Ingrid is sitting beside me on the bus, and her compliment is a meaningful one. She's never given me empty ones.

"It's funny that when we're finally getting enough snow to work on other stuff, I'm actually starting to get my slalom legs under me."

Ingrid laughs. "Yeah, but I bet you're still psyched about this storm. We're all itching to get onto other trails. You can only ski Rabbit Run so many times before you start to go a little nutso. Even I'm getting sick of running slalom gates, and they're my favorite."

"Will we do more drills and free skiing now? I mean, we don't always do gates, right?"

Ingrid pats my knee. "Sorry, Roxie. Your days of free skiing are over. You might be able to sneak in a run or two here and there, but the Morettis are pretty die-hard about running gates. We do a few drills outside that, but you must have known their coaching philosophy before you came here, right?"

"Kind of," I answer uncertainly. Gates, all day, every day? Is that really supposed to make the best skiers? It seems like a pretty narrow approach to me, but I guess they have the results to prove themselves. I'm not sure I believe Ingrid that I won't get to ski for fun once in a while. In the past, at least half my time on the mountain was spent free skiing, which just means not doing drills or gates.

We get off the shuttle in front of DH and my stomach roars to life. I'm hoping for spaghetti and meatballs tonight, when I hear my name and a very familiar squeal. I look up in time to see Chelsea

Radner barreling at me, arms wide. She jumps on me and I stumble until we're both lying in a pile of snow.

"Oh shit! Is that really you?" I ask.

"It's me, sister! I missed your cute butt and decided to come visit. Are you happy to see me or what?" She's sprawled on top of me, her round little face smack in front of mine.

"Chelsea, I'm thrilled you're here, but do you have to smother me?"

She winks before bouncing off. And before I can get all the way back on my feet, another body slams me back into the snow.

"What the--?"

There's a deep chuckle, one I've heard millions of times, and then the same arms that attacked me are pulling me up into a hug and onto my feet. "Hi Rox."

"Brad." I breathe in his comforting smell and give him a hard hug back. When I pull away, I have a glimpse of an audience gathering around us before another set of arms pulls me into him, and this time it's Tyler.

"It's not the same in Ashfield without you, Slade."

"I can't believe you guys did this. Well, I can totally believe it. This is awesome!" I'm screaming but I don't really care.

Ingrid is still standing on the sidewalk, her eyes darting around between my friends. People are hovering on their way to DH, wondering who these non-Stark kids are and why they're making a scene, but I only really care about Ingrid for the moment.

I introduce her to my friends, and it's nice that they seem to sort of know her already. She's heard about them a little too, but seeing her with them, still dressed in the long underwear and snow boots that all the alpine skiers hang out in after practice, I remember that Stark people are different. She didn't even know what a normal high school party was like, so she might not be super comfortable around my friends.

We catch up for a few minutes. They just got in, and flew right to Stark Springs. Their parents were more than happy to fly them out, I'm sure. There's snow here, so it's a training opportunity. Besides, I've always been known as the good kid in our group, so parents love me.

"We got a condo right on the mountain. Just in time for opening day! There's only one lousy trail open at Sugarville," Chelsea tells me. "So, what's the plan for dinner?"

"Oh, I usually go to DH but I don't know what the protocol is with visitors. Let's go to this pizza place downtown. Wait, did you guys rent a car? How did you find me, anyway?"

Tyler laughs. "We've been in touch with your roommate, Slade. She met us and gave us a tour and shit."

"What? Monica's been keeping this a secret from me too. That sneak," Ingrid huffs.

"Yeah, is the pizza place called Mario's?" Brad asks. "She's already there with your other friends."

"Misha and Liam?"

"Yup. Come on, girl, let's go." Chelsea links her arm in mine and then takes Ingrid's arm on her other side. "We got this huge-ass SUV. Good thing with the storm coming. Seats nine passengers and all our ski shit. Oh, and did I tell you we got awesome new fake IDs? We're gonna get loaded tonight."

"Better not be planning on doing it on campus. And quiet, you could get me in trouble." She's walking away now, but there are still a few lingering people watching us.

"Oh please, you aren't planning on getting wasted, are you?"

"That doesn't matter. And stop scaring Ingrid. No offense, Ingrid," I add. I'm sure talk of drinking freaks her out.

"That's okay. I want to see what normal high school kids are like."

Chelsea peers over at me with an odd look and we burst into laughter. Ingrid can be a little weird sometimes.

Brad beeps open a ginormous Chevy SUV and we pile inside. It's sort of cool that everyone has already met when we get to the restaurant. They seem to have hit it off, as far as I can tell. My friends refer to Monica and Liam as a couple, boyfriend and girlfriend, and I can tell by the way Monica beams that she is happy the status is official. I won't lie. I'm a little jealous. For the first time, I watch the two couples – Tyler and Chelsea and Liam and Monica – through a new lens. They're comfortable touching, leaning into one another, teasing and stealing each other's food. Ryker would never sit with me like that with this group. What was I thinking even suggesting something like that? Exclusivity basically means a relationship, and the idea is absurd with a guy like Ryker Black.

As if my thoughts have conjured him up, I see him enter the restaurant, the posse in tow. And he's headed straight for us with determination written all over his face.

Chapter 14

Aside from the first day at Stark, this is the first time Ryker has acknowledged me in public, or in front of the posse. Okay, there was the dance, and then the sledding session, but this feels different. The entire posse is with him, and he's now standing by our table, turquoise eyes flashing. Is he mad? My friends told Monica they were coming and if there was a rule against visitors or something, she would have known about it, right?

"Hi, Ryker." I hate that I sound nervous.

The table goes silent at his presence.

"You didn't tell me your friends would be visiting, Roxanne." Yeah, he sounds pissed.

I glance over at Monica, who's practically trembling. I shake my head, hoping she knows I wouldn't throw her under the bus.

"It was a surprise. They're here for the week, for Thanksgiving. Is that a problem?"

Brad is beside me, and I can feel tension rolling off him in waves. I've mentioned Ryker Black to my friends, and told them a little bit about his role on campus, but they didn't really understand, and I haven't told them about our meetings, the dance, the kiss last night. None of that. Brad, in particular, has been kept in the dark about Ryker, as I knew this is exactly how he'd react. And now that he's here in Stark, he's going to need an explanation or else he'll do something stupid. Shit. It might be too late for that.

Ryker doesn't answer my question, but introduces himself to each of my friends. Even Chelsea gets all rosy-cheeked around him. The posse has taken a nearby table, and they are watching us closely.

'Why don't you all come over to my place tonight? We're going to party and crash there."

My eyes dart around the table at his proposition. Ingrid, Monica, and Liam are gaping at him like he's lost his mind, and Misha is opening and closing his mouth like a fish. My Vermont friends look uncertain. They've heard about the posse, so they get that this is a strange offer, but I don't think they quite understand just how strange. This isn't like Ashfield and Sugarville, where everyone has an open invite to any party going on. It doesn't matter whether you go to the public school or the ski academy, if your parents are Olympians or you don't play any sports. At home, you just are who you are and no one cares about the rest.

Ryker must sense that no one is prepared to respond, so he continues, "With a foot of snow coming, there won't be practice tomorrow. They've got to groom the mountain, and it's supposed to keep dumping throughout the day."

I gather myself enough to say something. "That's, um, nice of you, Ryker, but my friends got a condo on the mountain so we were thinking about hanging out there." Before he can respond to me turning him down, I ask, "Will the lifts still be open? Does this mean we get a powder day without training?" Because that would pretty much rock my world. A powder day with my friends from home? Yeah, can't beat it.

"That depends," he says carefully.

"On what?" There's a challenge in my tone. If he thinks he can manipulate us into hanging out with him, he's got another think coming. He must know how incredibly awkward that would be.

"On the weather," he says, but his eyes say something different.

"You guys can come over to our condo," Chelsea offers, and I kick her under the table. Tyler grunts. Oh, I kicked Tyler. He tries to kick me back, but he must kick Brad, who snaps his head to Tyler.

I can't stop myself from laughing, and then Brad and Tyler realize what happened, and they join me. Ryker's response to Chelsea is drowned out by our laughter, but he doesn't look pissed. He looks smug as hell. Oh shit, he's coming over.

"We'll swing by after we eat." And then he turns and leaves to sit with the posse.

"Um, I didn't even tell him where we're staying," Chelsea says.

"He probably knows already," Liam explains.

"That was... trippy," Misha says slowly. "Did that really just happen? Are we partying with the posse tonight? Did Ryker Black just invite us *to his house*?"

"What is with that guy?" Brad ask. "You said he acted like he ruled the school, but what the fuck?"

"Relax, Brad." I place a hand on his arm. "I've figured out how to handle him. You'll get used to it. Just don't, like, piss him off, okay?"

Brad's jaw clenches. "You've got to be kidding me," he mumbles. "Who does he think he is?"

"He's a Stark," Tyler answers.

It takes a second, but I can see when Brad makes the connection. "Wait, Ryker Black is Elizabeth Stark's son? Well, fuck, that explains a lot."

We ask for a check around the same time that food is delivered to the posse's table, but our waiter says it's been taken care of. None of us bother asking who covered it. Ryker probably owns this restaurant.

When we pile into the SUV, no one says anything for a few minutes.

"Okay, Roxie." Ingrid speaks first. "You're the one who's been hanging out with him. Why did he want us to party with the posse? And why did he buy our dinner?"

"Wait, you've been hanging out with that guy?" Brad's pissed, that much is clear.

"Hardly." I feel it's important to downplay whatever has been going on with Ryker and me. I get the feeling he could be out of my life in an instant. And I still don't totally trust him. His intentions aren't exactly clear to me. "I've got no idea why he wants to party with us tonight or why he hangs out with me. He thinks he runs Stark, or maybe he really does, so my best guess is that I'm new and he wants to see what I'm all about. Maybe the same with the visitors."

"Oh shut it, Rox, you know it's because he wants your hot little bod," Chelsea calls out from the back of the SUV.

I groan. She doesn't get it. "Believe me, Chelsea, the guy can get any girl at Stark, he wouldn't go out of his way like this." I wish I could say he hasn't made a move, but after last night, that would be a lie.

Liam tries to explain Ryker's ways to Chelsea. "He wouldn't invite us to party with the posse just because he wants Roxie. It just doesn't work that way."

Tyler is the only one who doesn't seem fazed by it. "Who cares? Are they all tightasses like Black or are they cool? If they're chill it doesn't really matter to me why they're partying. Invite whoever."

All of my Stark friends protest that proposition immediately. If the posse is coming, the "rules" must be pretty clear that we are not to invite anyone else. Man, what a strange world I've joined.

"And as for buying us dinner, Ryker owns that place," Ingrid adds. Just as I thought.

We stop talking about the posse and Ryker when we get to the condo. My friends have already stocked the fridge with alcohol, and they must be planning on really getting after it this week judging by the amount in there.

Brad is tense as he pours a few shots, asking who all is joining him. Just Tyler and Chelsea, apparently. They don't push it. They're used to me not drinking, and I've told them that we don't get up to much shenanigans at Stark, so they know my Stark friends aren't into drinking.

There's a giant U-shaped couch in the living room area and some bean bags and we settle in and get comfortable, with Tyler setting up his phone to play some music from a set of speakers. It's no surprise they rented a pimped-out condo for the week, but it's still pretty cool we're here all alone without parents to answer to. Sure, I haven't had parents around for nearly three months now, but it's different when my Vermont friends are here. The training regimen and other weird rules about Stark make it almost more stifling sometimes. Now that we're off campus, it sort of feels like I'm back home being normal, just with a mix of Stark people and no parents. It's kind of awesome.

Chelsea's grilling Misha, Liam and Monica with questions about figure skating while Tyler and Ingrid talk shop about skiing. Brad is beside me and he nudges his knee with mine.

"We miss you, Rox," he says quietly. "*I* miss you. It's not the same back home without you."

His statements make me sad, and for the first time since I decided to come here, I feel guilty for my decision.

"I miss you guys too. Thanks for coming. It feels so good being around you again."

"Yeah? You're not forgetting about your small-towners?"

Is he *trying* to make me feel guilty? But he's smiling as he says it, only kidding around.

"You know I'll always be a small-towner, Brad. My friends here are good people, and the training is top-notch, but Stark will never be home."

"You haven't even gotten to ski the mountain yet, not really," Brad reminds me. "Wait until you ski the powder out here, Rox, it's nothing like powder days on Sugarville. The snow out west is lighter, it's not so dense. You'll see."

Talking about snow is easier than talking about people, and I almost forget we have guests arriving until they're standing around the kitchen a few minutes later, making themselves at home. The posse has come with loads of their own alcohol, and I glance at

Ingrid, Monica, Misha and Liam. They don't look uncomfortable or nervous, like I expect. I suppose if Ryker is here, in charge, then they don't feel like they're doing anything wrong, breaking any rules. I'm getting better, but sometimes I just forget that he's the king in these parts, and we are his subjects. It's so ridiculous.

Tyler's already gotten up to let them in, and he tells them to help themselves to whatever. He's always loved playing host. Chelsea seems fascinated by the posse, after what I've told her, and I can see she's studying them, wondering about all the things I've told her. It hasn't been much, just that they act like and are treated as royalty. Everyone wants the posse to approve of them, it seems. Even though the girls seem like bitches to me, I hear other girls talk excitedly when one of them throws a bone. It's so weird.

Since the episode at the dorm with Aspen and Winter, nearly a month ago now, I haven't had any run-ins with them. That's most likely because Ryker was out of town, and they had no cause to get all worked up about me hanging out with him, but what must they think about being here tonight? They said I'd never be friends with the posse guys, yet Ryker dragged the entire posse over here to party.

Ryker has found the shot glasses in the cupboard and he lines up a lot of glasses. Fourteen, I count. Enough for each of us. I watch from my spot on the couch. Brad gets up to start a fire, and the rest of my friends make their way over to the kitchen as Ryker pours whiskey into the shot glasses. It looks to me like he's done this many times.

He glances my way and our eyes lock. What is going on in that head of his? He's got the stormy expression, and I know he's challenging me, I just don't know what he's all about. Is this a threat, an ultimatum, a test of some sort? I know he's playing at something, I just don't know what.

He infuriates me.

"Let's start the night out right," he says to the entire room. His voice isn't loud, but even with the music playing in the background, it gets everyone's attention. Ryker holds up one of the shots and looks around the room. "To friends, and powder days." I'm not sure how to react when I watch everyone, even Ingrid, take a shot and hold it up, say cheers, and throw it back. Okay, Monica sips it tentatively, but this can't be Misha's first rodeo, because he doesn't even flinch.

I don't move from the couch. Brad looks my way as he takes a break from the fire to head over to the kitchen island. "Want me to take yours, Rox?"

But Ryker walks over to me at the same time, and offers me a shot. I take it, and glare at him. I don't want him thinking I'm doing this because he said so. As it so happens, I do drink once in a while, and I've even had shots of whiskey before. It's not something I do often, usually only on special occasions like birthdays or holidays, or, in this instance, my friends visiting.

Ryker tries to hold a steady expression when I toss it back, but his eyebrows lift just enough to tell me I've surprised him.

"No thanks, Brad, but you can pour me another."

Brad shakes his head at my antics.

"Oh, snap!" Chelsea calls out. "Are we getting wild Roxie tonight?"

I roll my eyes. I've been slightly drunk *maybe* three times. And Chelsea loves to get me all riled up. She's a very energetic person sober, and it only multiplies when she's in party mode.

With this kind of spirit to start out the night, it doesn't take long for the tension between the groups to thaw out. I'd imagined pure awkwardness between my Stark friends and the posse, but with Tyler, Chelsea and Brad here to bridge the gap, and a more than healthy dose of alcohol, everyone's getting along strangely well.

Word about what happened with Winter and Aspen must have been kept within the dorm walls, because as long as the three of us keep pretending they didn't assault and threaten me, no one else picks up on the way we are avoiding each other. I'll never really be friends with them, but I'll play along for whatever this is tonight.

I find myself sitting around the kitchen table with Sven, Player, Cody, Ingrid and Misha, playing spoons. It's the kind of game that takes all your attention, so I'm not really aware what everyone else is doing. A warm buzz is flowing through me, and I'm laughing as I wrestle over the last spoon on the table with Player. He wins, and I'm out for this game. These people are damn aggressive and apparently I'm not very sneaky because I'm the first to lose. Oh, well.

When I do finally tear my eyes away from the cards, I find two sets of eyes watching me from the couch on the other side of the room. It's an interesting sight. Brad is on one side, his brown eyes smiling at me in that comforting, warm way of his. He likes seeing me happy. Ryker is on the other side of the couch, and his gaze is quite the opposite. Cold and dangerous. Why do I get the feeling he's testing me? How can I rise to a challenge if I don't know what it is?

And then there's Petra, between them. She's sitting cross-legged, a glass of wine cradled in her hands, and she looks way older than eighteen. I'm not surprised that Telluride and Aspen are both sitting in front of the fire right in front of Brad, giving him those looks that say, I'm down for anything. I see that all the time at parties with Brad. I wonder how it will play out with him here all week. Do the same rules apply to an outsider? Will he hook up with all the posse girls and will they be okay with that?

And then the horrible thought occurs to me that Ryker might be with one of these girls tonight, and I'll have to know about it. Man, I'm so glad I stopped things from going further last night. I already feel kind of nauseated just thinking about the idea of watching him go off to some room with Petra.

When Petra gets up to go to the bathroom, I take the opportunity to steal her spot on the couch to check in with Brad. Fine, I want to be close to Ryker too, but I'm not about to make it obvious.

I plop down beside Brad. "So, you guys seem to have everything figured out. What's the plan for Thanksgiving? We aren't actually going to try to cook a turkey by ourselves, are we?"

Brad laughs. "Right, you know we can barely handle microwave popcorn."

"Hey! I can totally bake cookies," Chelsea pipes in from cuddling with Tyler on the other end of the couch.

"Careful, baking at altitude is different," Tyler tells her.

"How do you know that? You can't even toast waffles right."

"I guess those two are still bickering like a married couple, huh?" I ask Brad.

"I'm telling you Rox, it's been rough listening to them without you around. I'm the third wheel."

"Stop making me feel guilty, Brad." My tone isn't harsh, but there's enough bite that Brad pulls me in for a side hug.

"Relax. I just miss you."

"Besides, I seriously doubt you're a third wheel. There always seems to be a different girl with you guys when I call." It's true.

I should shut up, with Telluride and Aspen eavesdropping. Petra comes back from the bathroom and gives me a dirty look. I slide over closer to Brad, and I can't tell if she's pleased she'll have to squeeze in next to Ryker, or pissed that she doesn't have access to the new hottie in town.

Before Petra can sit between me and Ryker, he slides right up against me, so that she has to take his spot. It's such a blatant move, no subtlety there at all, that even Petra looks momentarily confused. And then pissed. The girl is always pissed.

"You guys should come to my place for Thanksgiving," Ryker says, turning to face me. "DH has a decent spread, but my dad's in town and we'll have the works."

My hands clench at this. What is he doing? Since when were we openly friends like this? Having Thanksgiving dinner together, and when his dad is in town, is something you do with close friends and family, and judging by the way Telluride and Aspen are gaping at us, this invitation is a big deal.

"What?" Petra squeaks. "You're inviting all of them?" She doesn't even try to hide her disgust.

"Ryker, you know that everyone's going to be there, right? My parents are flying in. Are you sure you don't want to check with, um, your dad or someone to make sure there's space?" It's sort of fascinating hearing uncertainty from Telluride Valentini, who's got to be nearly six feet of solid muscle, and has stunning violet eyes. And she must not get an approving look from Ryker because she practically cowers when she looks up at him.

"You know I don't answer to my dad, Telly. I'll invite whoever I want. I want Roxanne and her friends to come."

Brad takes the words out of my mouth. "Nah, we don't want to impose or stir up shit. We'll throw our own little shindig man, thanks though."

Ryker isn't having it.

"I'd like you to come, Roxanne." He says it so quietly, right in my ear, I'm not even sure anyone else can hear.

I'm thankful when the card table I abandoned breaks the tension by coming over and forcing everyone to consolidate so they can join us around the fire and on the couches. Everyone's getting hyped up about the storm outside and someone has started passing around the bottle of whiskey. When I get up to use the restroom, the room spins around me, and I know it's time to call it a night.

Someone steadies me with a hand on my hip and I assume it's Brad, but Ryker's voice is beside me, his body warm at my back, a moment later. I don't know how I know it's him before he speaks. "Careful, Roxanne. Alcohol hits harder at altitude."

It's not necessary, but Ryker keeps a hand at my hip as I make my way to the restroom.

"You planning on coming in with me?" We're around the corner and out of sight from the living room, and I realize my words have been construed as flirtatious as soon as they are out my mouth.

Ryker has my back up against the door, his face lowered, lips inches from mine. "Would you like me to?"

I shake my head, unable to form words. My hand turns on the doorknob and when the door opens behind me I stumble inside, shutting it in his face.

I've got to get ahold of myself, I think, as I sit on the toilet. I made it clear what I wanted last night, and I'm not going to change my mind. He can't take advantage of the situation tonight only to be with someone else tomorrow. Does he think because he's playing nice with my friends, I owe him something? As I scrub my hands at the sink, anger begins to simmer. Is he doing all this because I stopped him last night, and he doesn't like hearing no? Did I make it a challenge for him? Is that what this is all about?

But when I swing open the door, ready to call him out, it's not Ryker waiting for me, it's Brad.

"Come on, Rox, you're smashed." He hands me a glass of water. "Let's tuck you in so you're not too hungover to shred snow tomorrow, huh?" He holds me close to his side, and I'll admit I need the support as we go upstairs. I just can't decide if I'm relieved or disappointed that it's Brad putting me to bed, and not Ryker.

Chapter 15

A rustling noise and the sensation of another person nearby wake me up the next morning. Brad is rummaging through a suitcase, and I lean up on my elbows.

"Morning." My voice is rusty and I'm parched.

"Hey Rox, how you feeling?"

I glance around the room, remembering that Brad brought me up to sleep in his bed since the bed space would be limited with everyone crashing, and we'd shared a bed at parties on plenty of occasions.

"Like a rock. I didn't even hear you come in last night." I notice the other side of the bed is neatly made. "Did you even sleep in here?" Maybe he crashed with one of the posse girls.

Brad moves to sit on the edge of the bed. "Nope, slept on the couch downstairs so you could get your beauty rest."

Frowning at him, I ask the obvious question. "Why?" I mean, he can tell me if he slept with someone, that's never been an issue for us. "I don't care if you hooked up with one of the posse girls, Brad."

His face falls a little at my words, and I don't get it.

"I didn't, Rox. And you know that even if I had, I probably wouldn't have shared a couch with them when there's a perfectly nice bed available up here. You don't even snore." He smiles, but it doesn't reach his eyes.

Now I'm confused. "Right, so why the couch, dude?"

Brad shakes his head. "Ryker flipped his shit when he saw me coming up here to crash. He thought I was going to violate you or some shit. What is that dude's problem, Rox? Are you sure there's nothing going on with you two?"

"Wait, you didn't sleep up here because Ryker told you not to?" Great, he's already got my friends from home listening to his orders now too. I've barely even woken up, but my blood is boiling.

"Not really, it just wasn't worth a fight over. The guy was ready to throw punches, Rox. I told him I was just going to sleep and to chill the fuck out, but he wouldn't back off. When I tried to ignore him and kept going upstairs, he grabbed my arm, ready to take me on."

I shake my head, surprised at how easy it is to imagine the situation. "Ryker's cray-cray, Brad. I'm sorry. I can't figure out what his deal is."

"Did he think he was protecting your honor or some shit?"

I laugh hard at that. Right. Ryker, who can't even fathom fidelity with one girl. "No, he's just a controlling fucker."

"Or he's jealous. I think the guy wants you, Rox, bad." Brad gives me a mischievous smirk.

"Oh, he wants me," I agree with a similar smirk. "But only for sex, and you know me, that's not really how I roll."

Brad fist-bumps me at my virgin status. "What'd he think I was going to do? Come up here and wake you up after you'd been drinking and start humping you?"

"Wouldn't be the first time, buddy." I'm teasing, but it's kind of true. Twice now, Brad has come on to me when he's been drunk. The first time I was drunk too, but able to recognize we'd regret it in the morning. On that occasion, he didn't actually wake me up or anything, but we were sharing a bed at a party, since neither of us could drive. The second time he was really wasted, and I was totally sober and knew he didn't really know what he was doing. He was pretty easily redirected and I don't even think he remembers that time.

But Brad's chuckle isn't genuine. Instead, he looks sort of hurt and sad. We haven't ever discussed it before, but I figured it was something I could dig him about, since it was a while back.

The door swings open, and Chelsea jumps on our bed. "Ready to get on the slopes, or what? Have you looked outside yet?" She jumps off the bed and pulls back the curtains to reveal a complete whiteout.

"How many inches?"

"Four-fucking-teen." She's smiling so widely I can't help but return it, forgetting the awkward moment with Brad.

"Better get ready then," Brad says, taking a pile of clothes with him to the restroom to change.

"Dude." Chelsea crawls back onto my bed and speaks in a low voice. "He and Ryker were this close," she holds up her fingers an inch apart, "to brawling it last night. All over Brad crashing up here. It was heated as hell."

"Yeah," I say on a sigh. "So he said. Sorry, Ryker's got issues."

Chelsea gives me a knowing smile. "Don't tell Tyler, but it was kind of a turn-on watching them fight over you like that. Two smoking guys staring each other down? I'm pretty sure all the girls were hot and bothered when they finally simmered down."

I groan. "Everyone witnessed it?"

"Yeah, girl, only Monica and Liam had gone to bed at that point. We were raging it late last night. I think everyone else is still asleep. It's only like, 8:30 or something."

I'm glad Brad backed down, because I'm sure Ryker wouldn't have been the one to do it. This is so humiliating. But with the promise of fourteen inches of fresh powder, I'm going to forget about it, and hope that everyone else does the same.

I'm not going to lie. I want to know where Ryker slept last night, and when I find him already in the kitchen hovering over a pot of brewing coffee with immense intensity, just like he does everything, I'm a little disappointed I won't get a chance to find out. I mean, I could ask him, but I'm a little too proud for that. He made it pretty clear that he was going to do what he wanted, so why did he get on Brad's case last night? Because I'd been drinking?

He peruses my sleep attire lazily, but I know there's heat behind it, because Ryker doesn't do anything without purpose, I'm beginning to learn. I've borrowed sweats and a tank from Chelsea, since I never went back to my dorm to grab my things once I met up with my friends last night. He passes me a mug of coffee without speaking, and when I take a sip he looks smug.

"What?"

"I pegged you right as a black coffee girl."

"You probably are too."

"A black coffee girl?"

It's too early for another weird conversation with Ryker, where I'm never sure whether we're flirting or fighting or what. I step around him and open the fridge, checking out my breakfast options. Ryker tugs my hip in a quick motion, and my back is suddenly to his front, his lips on my ear. "I don't like it when you ignore me, Roxanne. But you know what I really don't like? You sharing a bed with another guy." His voice is simmering with something that's not control, not anger, but something else.

"Oh really? You don't have a say on either of those things, Ryker." He could, if that's what he'd chosen. But he said he wouldn't make any promises, so I'm not about to make any for him.

"What if I want to have a say?"

Brad's voice breaks us apart. "We've got blueberry Pop Tarts, Roxie." There's an edge there, and I'm reminded that he and Ryker didn't exactly make friends last night.

"Thanks Brad," I say, without looking at him. "They don't have those at DH. I've missed them."

Brad pulls a box down from the cupboard and places two in the toaster for me. I find the creamer in the fridge and hand it to him as he pours himself coffee.

"Careful, dude, don't put too much coffee in your creamer."

Brad winks, and then proceeds to fill his mug up at least halfway with creamer.

It's a weird morning, and that's because, well, because there's really not that much weirdness going on. One night of drinking and crashing at a condo together, and it's like these three separate groups of friends have always been friends. I totally don't get it. Just yesterday, there was an insurmountable barrier between the posse and everyone else at Stark, and my friends here had never even met my friends from home.

Aspen and Winter continue pretending like they didn't attack me a few weeks ago, and to be honest, I don't really care about them. It's not like I'm actually going to be their friend, but if we're going to cross paths, I don't really feel like stirring up drama.

We go our separate ways when it's time to go back to campus to get ready for skiing, and to drop off the non-skiers. Practice has been cancelled for everyone at Stark, according to Ryker, but the skaters don't ski, even on days like this one. Too much risk of injury, according to their coaches.

It's just five of us – me, Ingrid, Brad, Chelsea, and Tyler – shredding the powder all morning together, and I've never felt anything like it. Ingrid insists I borrow a pair of her powder skis, which are unlike anything I've raced on before. We have to adjust the bindings to fit my boots, but it's worth the effort. They're much wider, and I feel like I'm floating, or maybe surfing, even though I've never surfed before. A lot of the mountain is still roped off, but the trails that are open are covered in fresh snow, and it's fun to explore a new mountain and finally get off that damn Rabbit Run I've done hundreds of times in the last month.

It's late afternoon, probably our last run before the lifts close, and we're standing by a roped-off wooded area, contemplating whether it's worth it to go out of bounds. Ingrid is telling us not to, but Brad wants to at least check it out. "No one's been back here yet, and you guys have had tons of snow. There's probably a decent base under the freshies."

Sometimes it just looks like there's a lot of snow, but as soon as your skis sink through the powder, you hit rocks and tree roots. Unless it's a trail that's been consistently groomed, packing down the snow as it comes, you never really know what you're going to get, especially this early in the season.

"I don't know," Ingrid keeps saying. She says we rarely get an entire day off like this, so I know she wants to take advantage, but I have to agree with her.

"Go for it, guys," a familiar voice says casually and we watch a snowboarder ride past us, ducking under the ropes as he turns into the trees, spraying snow behind him.

Petra, Aspen, Sven and Player follow his lead, and the rest of us glance at each other, shrug, and then slip under the rope.

This is the best feeling ever, carving through open trees on untouched snow, knowing my friends are somewhere nearby and occasionally glimpsing one of them out of the corner of my eye.

A snowboarder comes out of nowhere, and I recognize the dark grey jacket as Ryker's just before he wraps his arms around me and we collide, falling into the snow together.

"You asshole." I shove him away, but he doesn't move much. His entire body is practically covering mine. "You did that on purpose."

He's smiling and he lifts his goggles up to rest on his helmet. Great, now I've got no defense from those damn eyes. "I've been wanting to kiss you again since I let you stop me on Thursday night, and I'm not going to wait any longer."

Before I can remind him why we stopped in the first place, he uses one hand to pull my own goggles away and the other to hold me steady before he claims my mouth with his. And I mean *claim*, because he's really making a point this time. There's no hesitation, tenderness or patience behind it. All passion and fervor, and I can't help but respond.

I'm not sure how long it takes before I come to my senses, but when he shifts his body above mine, I push him back and he stops.

"I'm making the promise you wanted, Roxanne," he says quickly, breathlessly, before I can get a word in.

"What? Why?"

He slides back, still strapped into his snowboard and kneeling, facing me. I'm leaning on my side, skis on, poles still hooked to my wrists.

"You've got me tied up in knots. I can't stay away. I've tried. As long as you let me, it'll only be you, Roxanne. That's what you want, right?" It might be the first time Ryker's truly asked me what I want before simply taking it. Well, he did take it, I guess, and then asked after.

"If you change your mind, you'll talk to me first, tell me?" I know better than to ask for more yet. We're hanging out as friends, with other friends, and he's promising not to be with anyone else. That's probably all I want for now, anyway. I'm still uncertain about Ryker Black and whether he *can* be anything more to me. But I won't share him while I've got him.

He nods, not looking away from me. "It should go without saying that it's the same for you. And this gives me a right to say that you'll keep your distance from Brad, Roxanne. You won't sit so damn close to him on couches and you definitely will not sleep in the same bed, no matter the circumstances."

It seems a moot point, with Brad only visiting, so I just shrug and nod. "Fine."

He raises his eyebrows and then leans down again, reminding me why I'm putting up with the most infuriating boy I've ever met.

Chapter 16

It's the strangest week of my life, I think. Probably even stranger than my first week at Stark. I keep wondering if there's something major I'm missing. The posse continues to hang out with my Ashfield and Stark friends every night. It's a vacation week from classes, and I thought it'd be filled with training instead, but with the snow coming down in record amounts, practices have been cancelled. I can't be annoyed that I'm missing an opportunity to go home, because it's the best skiing I've done in my entire life, and my best friends are here anyway.

We trade between the condo and Ryker's house each night, and the skiers and snowboarders stick together on the mountain. Practices resumed for all the other sports, since the snow doesn't really affect them. Even the Nordic skiers are back on the trails for training. Ryker sneaks kisses now and then, but it never goes further, and we go our separate ways each night when it's time to go to bed, even if all fourteen of us are sleeping under the same roof. No one else seems to know what's going on between us, and for some reason, I like it that way. I'm not sure I want anyone else's opinion about what I'm doing with Ryker anyway.

The posse girls flirt hard with Brad, but I'm surprised he doesn't reciprocate. Each girl is beautiful in her own way, even if all of them except maybe Telluride have been bitchy to me in the past, but I told Brad it was fine if he wanted to have fun this week. I know how he is, and it's not like he'll be betraying our friendship by doing his thing with them.

I'm not sure what will happen after Thanksgiving, when Chelsea, Tyler and Brad go home and classes and practice go back to normal. Will the posse ignore us again? We certainly won't have time to keep partying. I haven't had anything to drink since that first night myself, but I'm still staying up later than usual.

Going to Thanksgiving at Ryker's house doesn't seem quite as ridiculous by the time Thursday rolls around, but I still resist. I don't get why he would do it when inviting me means inviting seven other people as well. But my friends, even my Stark friends, are curious to get a glimpse into the rest of the posse's world, and once they resolve we're going, I decide to get on board. I'll admit, I'm eager for any insight into Ryker Black that I can get.

When we arrive and I find the house lit up spectacularly, the driveway lined with fancy cars, I'm questioning why Ryker told me to dress casually. I'd felt stupid asking, but needed to know beforehand whether this would be a formal deal. As we step inside, I see plenty of jeans and sweaters, but that's the only casual thing about the evening. There are caterers walking around with appetizers and champagne flutes, and the house has transformed into a holiday masterpiece since we were here two nights ago.

A man who looks nothing like Ryker introduces himself as Ted Black, and at first I think he must be another relative, but then Ingrid tells him it's nice to finally meet Ryker's father. I was expecting a separation between kids and adults, maybe we'd all hang in the loft and eat at the "kids' table" or something, but instead, I see Player and Sven mingling with the adults. We'd figured out that there would be a bunch of adults, including most of the parents of the posse members, and as we make our way through the house, I discover there are at least a hundred people here.

"Do you know who any of these people are?" Tyler asks as we take it all in.

"Nope."

"I know a lot of them," Ingrid says. "I don't *know* them, know them, but I've met some or recognize them. We are pretty much in the midst of everyone who matters in the ski industry. Well, not quite everyone, but the most important ones. And not just the ski industry, but other winter sports too."

We all look around for familiar faces, but I don't see any. "You mean the business side, I take it? I don't see any athletes I know."

"Some of them are retired. Look over there, that's Chet Preston. First American to get on the Olympic podium in the super-G."

She doesn't have to tell us any more. We might not know what he looks like nowadays, but everyone has heard of Chet Preston Productions. They make amazing ski films.

Ingrid is pretty clued in to the scene, and I'm reminded her family is in this industry, even if they aren't as influential as the ones in this room. She points out people and gives us short bios. Olympic committee members, ski and snowboard apparel legends, numerous retired world class athletes, the CEO of the NHL, a couple of world cup team coaches, among others.

"Anyone from figure skating?" Liam asks.

Ingrid points to one person but I don't recognize the name. Misha says, "Maybe the figure skaters have their own Thanksgiving party." But I think we all know that figure skating doesn't have quite the influence of some of the other winter sports. It just doesn't have as big a following as skiing, snowboarding and hockey. It gets great spectator coverage at the Olympics, but not as many people figure skate recreationally, and there aren't giant mountain resorts and tourist destinations backing it up, giving it a name.

"So, why are *we* here?" I ask the obvious question.

"I think it's because of you, Roxie," Monica says quietly. "I don't know why, but Ryker wants you to be part of his world. He has since that first day he asked you to sit at his table. Maybe once he realized you wanted to do your own thing, he thought he'd go about it differently."

A waiter walks by with a tray of champagne flutes and I snag one, draining most of it in one go. Brad takes my arm and leads me down a hallway and away from everyone. I let him, grateful for the reprieve, but his brown eyes carry a storm when he finally faces me.

"I don't like this situation with Ryker Black, Rox." He speaks quickly, looking around like he's afraid we'll be overheard. "I know we've been hanging out with him all week, and it's been fine or whatever, but I don't trust him with you. The way he looks at you, Rox..." Brad stops and closes his eyes.

"How does he look at me?" I really want to know what Brad sees.

"He watches everything you do. Look, I know you already know that he's not like other eighteen-year-old kids, but the more I've talked with his friends, the more I realize that he's actually someone with a shitload of power."

"Yeah, I know," I say slowly. We've been over this before. What's different now?

"I think he's dangerous, Rox. I don't think that everything these people do," Brad gestures in the direction of the party, "is legit. Ever since you started mentioning the weirdness at this place, I've done some more digging around, throwing out names and asking questions around Sugarville. People are scared of Ryker Black, Rox."

"What people? I mean, I know Monica and Ingrid and everyone at Stark is scared of him, but..."

Brad interrupts me. "Rox, I asked Jim Castle -- you know the dude who owns Sugarville Mountain, my dad's buddy? I asked him if he knew Ryker Black, before I knew Ryker was a Stark, and he did. He said he does business with him, and you don't want to cross that guy. He talked about him like he was a colleague, not a fucking junior in high school."

He's speaking quietly, and I'm trying to process what he's saying. I mean, this isn't *totally* shocking information. It's not like I hadn't listened to Ryker talk to his buddies about his business trip, but I'd sort of assumed he was going as his dad's sidekick, like to shadow him and start to get a feel for the family business, get introduced to people, begin to learn the ropes. It was plausible that he was acting as a student representative for the academy. I didn't think the owners of other ski mountains would really treat him like an associate, someone who "you don't want to cross."

Before I can respond to Brad, we turn at the same time to the sound of someone walking quickly down the hallway in our direction. Ryker looks angrier than I've ever seen him, and I suddenly notice how close Brad is standing, that he's holding my arm, bent toward me. It could definitely be interpreted the wrong way, and I take a step back, putting distance between us. It's too late, and only makes the conversation look guiltier than it is. Oh wait, there *is* something to be guilty about.

Brad gives me a look that says, *See what I mean?* Ryker does look pretty scary right now, but powerful too, and even though it shouldn't, it makes me want him to whisk me away and kiss me like he has been doing all week.

"Walk away, Brad," Ryker says darkly. "Roxanne and I need to speak privately." His teeth are clenched, and I know he's exercising restraint. He doesn't make a direct claim to me, or say that I'm his girl and Brad shouldn't be alone with me, hovering close in a dark corner. But his body language does send that message, and Brad doesn't question it. He walks away, leaving me alone with the guy he just warned me about.

"We need to talk." Ryker and I say the words at the same time, but neither of us finds any humor in it. He takes my hand and pulls me into an office.

"I thought we had an agreement, Roxanne. You promised me." Ryker's voice almost cracks, and there's more than a hint of vulnerability. Do I have power over him?

'We do. I was just talking, Ryker."

Ryker paces over to a built-in bookshelf, his back to me, and then he turns around and stomps back, and I know he's going to kiss me but I put my hand up to his chest, stopping him.

'If we're going to keep doing this, I need you to tell me who you are, Ryker. Why are people scared of you? Why do you hold so much authority over the Stark students?" I'm not sure exactly what I'm asking, but he seems to understand better than I do.

He heaves a few breaths, and I can't tell if he's annoyed, angry, or what. It's like he's trying to steady himself, like I've thrown him off with my questions.

"You really don't know, do you?"

"Know what, Ryker?" I ask impatiently.

"I'm the CEO of Stark, Inc. Officially since my eighteenth birthday but unofficially for several years now."

My mouth is hanging open, but I can't seem to shut it.

He smiles softly, and then closes it with his index finger.

I have about five hundred questions, but I don't question the truth of what he's said. For some reason, I believe it. "What about your dad?"

Ryker looks away. "My dad's weak. He lost it when my mom died, weeping all the time and barely able to dress himself, let alone run a multi-billion-dollar corporation."

"So, what happened?" I mean, there must have been alternatives besides a kid. He was twelve when his mother passed away.

"My mom's brother, Uncle Will, he never had much interest in the business. It became clear early on that he was the athlete in the family, and my mom wasn't. Will was the Olympic skier and my mom became the businesswoman." Ryker speaks about it so casually, like it's just a given that everyone in the Stark family is exceptional in some way.

"After my mom passed, there was a shitstorm for a few years with people fighting for position, but Stark has been a family business for over two hundred years, and that wasn't going to change. At least not officially. I'd always been interested in my mother's work, and I started reading my dad's emails, checking his messages, keeping up with what was going on. The board gave him some time to grieve, but they were losing patience, and I wasn't even a consideration. But then I started basically pretending to be him, learning about the business and giving authority to do shit."

"You were twelve." I'm not sure I can believe him now. It's too absurd. What was I doing when I was twelve? My parents wouldn't even let me watch R-rated movies.

"No, by then I was fourteen. Look, I didn't really do anything major, I just kind of copied the way the other people spoke to each other on email, and I'd look up the things they were talking about. It was pretty fucking fun, actually."

"You can't be serious."

"By the time I was sixteen, my dad, Uncle Will, the board, half the industry figured out what was going on. Anyone who challenged it or questioned it, got screwed over."

I start to ask what that means, but he doesn't let me.

"My dad let me do what I wanted. He started taking orders from me, just like he used to from my mom." Ryker sounds disgusted. "I need to get out there," he says, changing gears before I can ask him anything else, though my head is swimming with questions. "I've got a lot of people to speak with this evening, Roxanne, and I don't want to be worrying about you running off with Brad," he says darkly.

Why does he even care about that when he's an eighteen-year-old CEO of one of the most powerful corporations in the world? It's so... trivial. I feel very small. My entire life seems incredibly insignificant. My dislike for Petra, my reaction to Lia's coaching, all of it just dwindles in importance compared to Ryker and the things he does. The people he employs. The decisions he makes and the consequences they have. I start to feel a little dizzy.

He steps closer. "Are you okay?"

I clear my throat and try to smile. "Yeah, that was just, quite the revelation."

"Can I kiss you now?" he murmurs, his head already lowered, his mouth almost on mine. But I like that he asked. So I nod, and he does. I think he might find comfort here with me, I don't know. But he kisses me as if he cherishes this moment of hiding away.

Ryker and I split up as soon as we leave the office, and I'm in my own head for the rest of night. There's a buffet dinner for the actual meal, and I stick with my friends, catching glimpses of Ryker speaking to various people throughout the evening. A tiny piece of me is flattered that he's shown an interest in me, now that I know how big his world is. But the rest of me is entirely overwhelmed. I'm confused beyond belief, and I know there's got to be more to what he's telling me. There must be. I feel quite distant from him as more unanswered questions pop into my head. Why does he even go to Stark? What's the point? He doesn't need school. How can he actually be doing what he says and training at a world-class snowboarding level? None of it seems real. And I'm feeling kind of sick.

Most of my friends are star-struck and in awe, just taking it all in: the food, the decorations, the people. But Brad is watching me closely; I can feel his eyes on me. I've got an unbearable urge to just escape. Remembering a bathroom on the second floor, I sneak upstairs to get away. From behind a closed door, the sound of Aspen's voice stops me as I walk down the hallway. She's speaking to her father.

"Dad, he cancelled training for five days. *Five* days. He's never done anything like that before. He did it for her, because her friends were visiting, and I think he thought she needed a break from training. She can't handle it here, and he doesn't treat her like anyone else."

"Darling, maybe he just likes her. It's nothing to get worked up about. It will run its course, as these things do."

"You're not listening to me, Dad!" I almost laugh at her whiny voice, but the words she's uttering make the sick feeling in my stomach grow. "Ryker doesn't do things like this for no reason. You need to find out who she is and why she matters. She must have connections we don't know about."

"She doesn't, Aspen. She's just another talented athlete. He's spotted them before and he's been right. You know he recruited Ben Quincy to Stark and look how that turned out. He's the top scorer in the NHL his second year in. Ryker doesn't just have excellent business intuition, he's got an eye for athletic talent."

"I know, Dad. Ryker's a prodigy. That's why I don't get why he would be interested in a girl like Roxie Slade."

I hurry away, having heard enough. I don't understand it either, and once again, I'm left wondering if there's something big I'm missing here. Why me?

Chapter 17

Chelsea, Tyler and Brad leave the day after Thanksgiving. I'll see them in less than a month for Christmas break, when I get a week off to go home. Still, I find myself fighting tears when we hug our goodbyes in front of my dorm. So much has changed this week, and I don't know if things will ever be the same for me at Stark. I know that my friends are aware that hanging out with the posse all week was an unexpected turn of events, but I don't think any of them have contemplated what will happen once they leave and go back to Vermont.

Brad is the last to say his goodbyes, and when he hugs me, I realize that maybe he has thought about my life at Stark once he's gone. "You know that if things get too hard for you here, you can always come back to us, Rox."

"I'm not a quitter, Brad."

"No, you're not, but sometimes there are just better alternatives. You have a choice, you know?" He pulls back from our hug and looks right at me, and I wonder if he's talking about something aside from where I train, or where I live and go to school.

For the first time in a week, I don't see Ryker for an entire day after Thanksgiving. We're back training with Rocco and Lia, and I wonder if what Aspen said to her dad was true. Did he cancel practices for me? Because he thought I needed a break from training? It's hard to believe he would care about me and my well-being enough to alter everyone's training regimen for an entire week. I'm well aware now how unusual even one day off is.

After the Thanksgiving party, I only catch glimpses of Ryker on the mountain or around campus, I'm fairly certain our next conversation will be him telling me it's over between us.

But no, he takes me by surprise, which seems to be his way.

I'm the last one to leave the classroom after English, having just sent off a text to my parents. I hear the teacher greeting Ryker in the hallway before I see him, and then he's in the classroom with me, shutting the door behind him.

"I've missed you, Roxanne," he says simply. Now would be the time to return the sentiment, but I'm a little angry with him for ignoring me for three days after the week we spent together.

"Why did you stay away, then?"

A smile slides across his lips. "Why? Are you upset that I did?"

Sighing, I try to walk around him. "I'm not in the mood for this, Ryker.

He swipes his arm out and pulls me to him, so I'm standing between his legs while he leans back on a desk. "Not in the mood for what, Roxanne?" His eyes search my face, as if he really doesn't know the answer to his question.

"I don't know what we are, what this is," I say, gesturing between us. "You hang out with me and my friends all week, you invite us to Thanksgiving, and you start to open up to me about who you are, your life and your past. And then you don't speak to me for three days with no explanation."

"I'm sorry. I did tell you that it would be less complicated if we made no promises to each other." When I start to pull away at that he holds me tighter. "I'm not breaking any promises to you, Roxanne. I didn't get in touch because I've been very busy. You now know why I am so busy. Many of the Thanksgiving guests have been in town through the weekend, and I had meetings, as well as practice resuming."

Which reminds me. "Why did you cancel practice all week? You are the one who made that happen, aren't you?"

He looks down before answering. "Because it was some of the best snow we've had in history, and I thought it would be good for morale and perhaps even general fitness if the athletes just enjoyed free skiing and free riding for a few days. It's still very early in the season. Now, how are you feeling about your first race next Saturday?"

"Excited, I guess."

"Good. Can I kiss you now, Roxanne?"

I answer by leaning forward, letting him in. I don't know what we're doing, not exactly, but at least when we *are* together, it feels right.

The next two weeks leading up to our first race fly by. Ryker checks in every couple of days, always getting me somewhere alone. He asks how things are going, and then kisses me, and then leaves. I don't get a chance to find out much about what's going on in his world, and the meetings are always on his terms. He continues to ignore me and my friends at DH, on campus, and on the slopes, just as he always had before, and the rest of the posse follows his lead. I can't decide if this is the ultimate diss or if it's a huge relief to remain out of the social hierarchy.

Misha, Liam, Monica and Ingrid seem to share my mixed emotions. Yeah, we actually had fun during that strange week, but partying every night like that isn't real life, and without my Vermont friends, the balance is totally thrown off. It's for the best that the posse is back to ignoring us so we can just focus on training. Still, rejection of any kind is a little painful and it makes me wonder, as I imagine my friends do too, if the posse does this kind of thing on a regular basis and we just never hear about it. Maybe they infiltrate groups of friends for a week or two of partying every once in a while, just to spice up their social lives while keeping it all in check and under control, and then act like they don't even know the people afterward. Who knows? And really, who cares? It's only Ryker's involvement in the whole thing that keeps me thinking about it.

We've been training GS gates since Thanksgiving, and I've got to say, I'm feeling damn good about myself going into my first race as a Stark athlete. Rocco's the main coach on GS and, like Lia with slalom, he doesn't like to use a stopwatch on us except for race day so I can't say anything for sure about how I'm comparing to everyone. Still, after my breakthrough day on slalom, I've not only been more confident, but more intentional about going after it, trying to prove that I'm not weak, that I really do want to be the best I can be.

Stark is hosting a scrimmage of sorts for our first "race." It's not an official race under the FIS (Federation International du Ski), but more like a warmup race against other Colorado ski academies. Our results don't officially count for anything, except our pride.

The hierarchy for ski racing levels starts with high school, which is public high schools, and most Stark racers would win those on one ski. Then it's USSA (United States Ski Association), FIS, Nor-Ams (or Europa Cup if racing in Europe), and the highest level is World Cup. Like most people at triple-S, I'd been racing USSA level until last season when I started racing FIS. If your point are low enough, you can go to Nor-Ams races. All Nor-Ams and World Cup races are under the FIS point system. The crazy thing about ski racing is that once you hit FIS level, there are no age groups. This first race is a rare opportunity to race only high school-aged racers, even if they are way above "high school" level racing.

My results at the first race are good. Not amazing, and not terrible. Solid. Seventh place, with four Stark racers ahead of me, and two from other Colorado teams. I'm pleased to be in the mix, but I want to do better. For such a small, low-key meet, it was tough competition.

As I'm leaving the training hut later that afternoon, I hear someone crying, and find one of the seventh graders who was on my tour that first day sitting on a bench by the lockers. Carla, the one who wanted a selfie with Player. Today, her eyes are red-rimmed.

Sitting down beside her, I put an arm over her shoulder. "Want to talk about it?" We don't really know each other, since she trains with the younger group at a different time of day from me, but sometimes it's easier to talk to someone who's not very close, just another teammate.

She wipes her eyes and takes a deep breath. "I'm not going to make it to Christmas." Her voice is calmer than I expect. Sad, but resolved.

"What do you mean?"

"I almost got last place today, Roxie. Stark athletes never finish in the bottom half at any kind of race, you know that. It's a rule. Unless something catastrophic happens, but then you're better off with a DNF."

It's true, if your ski catches a gate or you take a tumble, it's generally better for your rankings to ski off the course and take a "Did Not Finish" over a poor placing.

"Did something happen or did you just have a bad race?"

"Nothing happened. I'm just not fast."

"Well, you got in to Stark for a reason, Carla, I'm sure that's not true."

"I got in because my parents went here. My father's on the Olympic Committee and my mother's side of the family owns Veldo." Veldo is the hottest company for all things snowboard-related. "I've always been a pretty good ski racer, so they gave me a chance, but I'm not cut out for Stark. It sucks."

She starts crying again and I pull her in for a hug and then she really gets sobbing, all over my jacket, gasping in breaths. I remember when I cried once after taking a DNF at the USSA state meet in eighth grade. I'd lost control and missed a gate in the GS, which I'd won for the past four years. Though I haven't cried from a bad race since then I did feel like crying after my first day of training at Stark, so I can relate to the need for a good old-fashioned pity party.

I give her the best reassurances I can about working hard, not giving up, and believing in yourself, but I don't think she's really listening.

I find myself thinking about Carla a lot over the next few days. She didn't think she was good enough for Stark, and assumed she'd gotten in because of her parents. I can totally relate to feeling like a mistake at Stark, that I'm not good enough, that I'm not supposed to be here. But at least I know it was my racing and not my parents that got me in. As the weeks have turned into months, and I've had more experiences on and off the mountain, I'm feeling less and less like an outsider. And after the race on Saturday, I'm beginning to think that I'm right where I belong. It's only early in the season, and I'm already in the mix with the other Stark racers, not behind at all.

But when I find out that Carla has left Stark, and won't be returning, my insecurity comes rushing back.

I'm riding on the lift with Ingrid when she brings it up.

"She's not the first to go, Roxie, don't get yourself worked up about it."

"But, did she get kicked out? Why did she leave?"

"We don't talk about these things, Roxie, but it should be obvious. She wasn't good enough. They probably let her in as a legacy who had great connections, hoping she might rise to the challenge, but she just doesn't have what it takes to be a great skier. Stark can't make exceptions like that, no matter who you are. It's an embarrassment having a Stark athlete finish second to last place."

"But it was her first race, and it wasn't even an important one. They can kick you out for that?" I'm seriously outraged on Carla's behalf, because, well, that could so easily have been me.

"She didn't exactly get kicked out. It doesn't usually work that way. Usually the teammates and coaches are just super mean and harsh until the person can't take it. But Carla knew it was coming. She was already packing her bags before shit got real."

I'm shaking my head, close to tears over a girl I hardly know. "That's so messed up."

"This is Stark, Roxie. Carla knew it when she came. She'll still go to a nice school, probably even a ski academy, and do well. She's a good racer, a cool girl. It's not like her life is over."

It's true, Carla comes from money, and this wasn't her only shot at success, but getting kicked out after making friends and training hard, living here for three months? That's rough. Besides, I'm sure it's a shameful thing to come home with her tail between her legs after her parents graduated from Stark and have friends in this world. It would suck for me, and my friends and parents would love to have me back home. I just have to hope Carla's confidence isn't permanently damaged.

I can't shake it though, the thought that her friends and teammates would have turned on her, maybe even had, just because she didn't race well. I look at the coaches, and wonder how they can be harsh to a thirteen-year-old. That's what Ingrid said, that basically they would have, or did, tear her down until she couldn't take it anymore. And now I understand what Petra was telling Ryker to do the other day in the locker room. She thought he should be mean to me, try to break me, and not build me up. And why didn't he?

When I walk by the posse's table that night, I'm fuming. They're all sitting there, laughing, acting untouchable. And Ryker, who doesn't even look my way as I breeze past him, he's the one controlling all of it. Ruining lives from his almighty throne. It really pisses me off. I'm not sure why I do it, but I just can't let it go.

So I backtrack and plop my tray down between Winter and Ryker, pulling up a chair from a nearby table. Their laughter stops, and the noise in DH goes from boisterous to near silence in seconds. The attention on me, on this table, only gets me more fired up. And then I let loose.

"So, Ryker," I say slowly, "are you the one who decided Carla should get kicked out? Or was it you, Petra? Of course, Ryker had to give the stamp of approval, right?"

Petra looks a second away from attacking me, but she's waiting on Ryker.

"You guys think just because you have everything you could possibly want, that it's your job to play with people's lives who don't have it all?"

Ryker grabs my arm. "Roxanne." His voice is low and threatening, but I'm not listening. I had no idea I had so much rage building up inside me, but it's all coming out, and it can't be stopped.

"And you, Ryker, you think you're too important to say hello or even look at people you pretended to be friends with? What is your problem? How many other girls around here are you kissing and ignoring? Are you ashamed of me? How many other dirty secrets are you keeping?"

"Enough," he growls, pulling me up by arm and dragging me away. "You know nothing, Roxanne. Just drop it."

I shake him off but continue outside, the same way he's going. All of a sudden, I can't stand this place and the scared little eyes watching me are so stifling I want to scream.

Thankfully, no one follows us outside and we're alone in the cold night air, so I do scream. "What is wrong with everyone here? Why do they do everything you want? What are they so scared of?"

"Just accept it, Roxanne. Stop questioning it. It's like I said that first day. There are rules, and everyone has been following them for a very long time. If you don't like it, leave. If you can't pull your weight in your sport, we make sure you do leave. It's simple." He sounds so detached, so controlled, I want to throw him off, but I don't think I have that kind of power over him.

We have a long stare-down, and I resist the urge to shove him. "I don't understand this world. I don't like it." I wait until I'm calm enough before I say it. "I want to ski race, but at what cost? I won't ever terrorize another teammate into leaving just because they're not as fast as I am. If that's what it takes, I'm out of here."

"You do understand this world, Roxanne, you just won't accept it. It's your decision. We're not forcing you to stay. But most people fight to be here, and I thought you'd be a fighter. It's worth the reward, if you're willing."

"Why the games, Ryker? Why act like our friends one day and refuse to acknowledge us the next? What does that have to do with making the best athletes?"

Ryker looks away. "Spending time with you all week was a mistake."

My stomach lurches at his admission. "Why, then?" My throat is tightening, but I get the words out. I have to know what his game is.

"I told you the truth, I never lied. I wanted to spend more time with you, and I didn't trust Brad. If you were going to be with him all week, I wanted to be there too."

I laugh at that. "Well he doesn't trust you, either."

Ryker's eyes flash darkly. "I let my emotions, my personal wants and desires get in the way, and it wasn't smart. I wanted insight into your life. Your life here at Stark and your life before you came. It was foolish."

I let out a frustrated noise. "Why do you always have to be so cryptic? Just spell it out, Ryker. That doesn't explain why you and your friends in there have to ignore us as if we never hung out together. It's not only rude, it's hurtful."

"Don't you see it's more than training and racing? I've been trying to tell you that, Roxanne. It's why I don't make promises, though I've kept mine to you. We need order, structure, and even fear, to work the way we do." He steps closer and speaks quietly. "I won't maintain my position if I show weakness. I can't hold the power I do, especially at my age, without intimidation. Showing any vulnerability, particularly when there's an easy target like a person involved, is not an option in my world. So if you think for one second you're going to be my girlfriend, you need to get over it."

He's less than a foot away, nearly touching me. I'm not sure what to feel, and there are too many emotions warring inside of me to make sense of them. The strongest one is sadness. I never thought it possible, but I almost pity Ryker in this moment. He sees life as a game, and he's just another player. People are weapons to be used against each other, pawns in a strategic effort to gain the most, beat the others. At least, I think that's what he's saying.

And he can't let it be any other way, or he won't allow it. For some strange reason, I think of what he told me about his mother, and I wonder if she's why he's like this.

'It doesn't have to be the way it's always been, Ryker. You could change it if you wanted." And then I echo what Brad said the day he left. "It doesn't make you a quitter. It just means you're choosing a better alternative."

Chapter 18

Monica doesn't come home to the dorm that night until I'm already in bed, and she leaves early the next morning for practice, before I'm even awake. It's like she's afraid of me, and I hate it. Ryker went back into DH without another word after our conversation, and I'm not sure what to expect from him. Are we done? We've both presented each other with choices, but just as I'm not about to accept the way things are run at Stark and what that means for my non-relationship with Ryker, he's equally unlikely to change.

The final pieces of the Ryker Black puzzle are falling into place. Ryker was raised by an ice queen, and when she died, his father wasn't there for him, or for Stark, Inc., leaving Ryker to fill both his parents' shoes. I will never know what that was like. Watching him interact with everyone on Thanksgiving, I could see that he's almost more comfortable amongst adults, business moguls and coaches or world-class athletes with exceptional talent in other fields. He fits in with them, and struggles to fit in with those of us who are his own age, here at Stark. He doesn't understand how to relate to his peers, instead trying to maintain order with the posse and in his relationships, as if we are all part of the corporate world he threw himself into at age twelve, or fourteen, or whenever it was.

The last people I feel like dealing with today emerge from the common area just as I'm about to leave the dorm for breakfast.

Petra speaks first. "Roxie, we need to talk."

I glare at her. "About what?"

"We want to apologize."

I huff out a laugh. "Right. Did Ryker give you permission to do it or are you going rogue?"

"Ryker doesn't control everything we do, Roxie," Petra replies. She sighs. "Look, I know I haven't always been nice to you, but I didn't understand why he wanted a new athlete to come on the team as a junior. But he made the right call and I've accepted it."

I cross my arms. "You aren't here to get back at me for calling you out last night at DH?"

Aspen giggles and then nods in approval. "You only did it because Ryker's been doing his usual ignoring thing, acting like a jerk, and you were brave enough to confront him on it. It was coming to him, and we've all been in your shoes."

That doesn't make me feel any better.

Winter steps forward then. "We know we told you to stay away at first, but we actually really liked hanging out with you, and we thought Ryker was finally going to expand our group. When he stopped hanging out with you and your friends after Thanksgiving, we tried to change his mind, but screw him. I think we should be friends, and show him that we don't have to do everything he says."

I eye the three of them skeptically. "Right, you want to be friends with me and with my friends after first being rude, then assaulting me, and then ignoring us? What's your game?" Game. Is it always a damn game?

"We like what you did at DH, Roxie," Petra says. "We think it's time to change things around here. Be friends with who we want, show everyone that the Stark legacy doesn't have power over everything we do."

I'm not sure I believe these girls, after what they said before, but it's not like they can hurt me. Only Ryker really has the power to play with my emotions, so if they want a truce, fine. It will be easier than them giving me hell.

"Well, what do you want?" That's the question, isn't it?

"Just to hang out. Ryker's left on business again, so it's not like he can have a say about it anyway," Petra tells me.

"We're going snowmobiling and night skiing tonight, right girls?" Aspen looks between her friends. "Let's invite Roxie. Want to come?"

I'm not so sure. "I'll think about it."

The girls tell me when and where we can meet, and indecision preoccupies my thoughts during classes and practice. Would this be a betrayal to Ingrid, Monica, Liam and Misha? I'm sort of annoyed with them and their constant fear of Ryker. I wish they'd stand up for themselves and challenge the posse; it'd be nice to have their support. But that's sort of what Petra, Winter and Aspen have offered, isn't it? They're extending an olive branch as a way to show that they aren't totally on board with Ryker's whole intimidation and fear regime, that they're willing to defy him and hang out with people he's deemed not good enough.

So I show up at the parking lot ready to ski that evening, having decided that, at the very least, I'll get a chance to ride a snowmobile for the first time. What's the worse they can do? Push me off a cliff?

Turns out they're a little more creative than that.

***

The girls drive about twenty minutes away from campus in the opposite direction of the resort before unloading the snowmobiles. Though they are acting normal, I've got my guard up. I'm already wondering if it was a mistake not to tell anyone where I was going, but I just didn't want any judgment. If this is some sort of opportunity for me to hash it out with Petra, Aspen and Winter, once and for all, I'm up for the challenge.

Winter explains that she likes to get out on her snowboard sometimes, but no one except the posse knows about it, so to keep it on the down-low. The coaches don't want skaters risking injury, and they'd be furious.

It's already beginning to snow when we load our skis and snowboards onto the snowmobiles. I'm sharing one with Aspen, and as we wind our way up a mountain I've never been to before, the gentle snowfall turns into a blizzard. The snowmobile headlights show us the way, and I'm glad I brought my headlamp, though the visibility will be rough skiing in the dark in a blizzard even with light.

I'm not sure how long we drive, Aspen leading and Petra and Winter on a snowmobile behind us, but eventually Aspen slows the snowmobile, and turns to me with a grin. "Ready for the best night skiing ever?" She might be right, even considering that night with Ryker that she doesn't know about. Here in the middle of nowhere, with snow dumping on us, it's going to be one hell of an adventure.

I pull my goggles up to get a better look at the slope below as I slide off the snowmobile. There's nothing like fresh tracks; no matter what else happens tonight with these girls, at least I'll get a sweet run. But when I look up, ready to unload my skis, Aspen is pulling away, along with Petra and Winter.

"You didn't really think we wanted to be your friend, did you?" Aspen taunts.

No, I didn't. But the words don't come. I just stare back at them, stunned at their cruelty.

"Ryker never wanted you, Roxie," Petra calls out, remaining twenty feet away. Do they think I'm going to run after them in snowboots and tackle them off the snowmobiles? Tempting, but I'm suddenly resigned to the stunt they're pulling. "It was all a game. You never should've challenged him, challenged the posse. He's always looking for an opportunity to set an example, and you were the perfect, gullible target. As soon as you got to be too much of a handful, acting all clingy, and getting in our face at DH like you did, it was time to pull the trigger."

A surge of shame washes over me as her words sink in. I'm just another Olga Popova, after all.

"It's always been a game," Winter says what I already know. "And it always will be. Have fun finding your way back!"

And with a roar of engines, the snowmobiles disappear into the night. Immediately, I check my cell phone, and I'm not surprised to find that there is no service. Not allowing myself to dwell on the crushing layer of embarrassment, hurt, anger, and loss, I begin in the direction the snowmobiles went, sinking into the deep snow with each step. My ski boots are heavy, and it's slow going. It's some time later when the battery on my headlamp dies, and then I realize the tracks have crossed each other, and the girls must have gone in circles, either for kicks, or to purposefully throw me off, or both, I don't know. But by now, the snow has mostly covered the tracks anyway, so I decide my best bet is to travel downhill, where I'm likely to meet Route 541, the road we took from Stark.

As I stumble downhill, falling onto my knees on more than one occasion, my thoughts are all over the place. I'm too angry to cry, and I won't give them that satisfaction anyway. Not that they're watching, but it's the principle of it. No one even knows I'm out here, except for the girls who put me here. And Ryker. Ryker Black. This was all a test. I was a pawn in his game, and I didn't even know it. I suspected it, yes, I always got the feeling I was missing something, but this? I never imagined it'd go this far.

It would've been an epic ski run, I think miserably as I slide on my butt and grab a tree, narrowly missing a not-so-small cliff into a ravine. What if I die out here? Will anyone figure out what happened? It's been hours, and still no sign of civilization.

How could I be so stupid? Monica warned me. Ingrid warned me. The girls who did this even warned me. Hell, Ryker told me that very first day, minutes after I arrived, that I had to play by his rules. Why did I think I could be an exception? I should have listened to my instincts when I first drove through Stark and arrived on campus. I don't belong here. I should be home in Ashfield, trying to navigate classes at Sugarville High while getting over to the mountain to train whenever I can. I should be with my parents, helping out at the general store, and hanging out with my friends, who don't have any hidden agendas, whom I trust unconditionally.

Maybe I should even be with Brad, like he's always wanted, but never outright said to my face. I've tried to deny it, but now that I'm all alone, freezing, hungry, and heartbroken, the truth is staring right at me. Brad's always wanted more with me, he was just waiting for a sign. Maybe if I go home, things will change between us.

But several hours later, when I finally see a flash of light, and realize I'm nearing a road and that I might not die, after all, I make a decision. I'm not leaving Stark. Not this year, at least. I'm going to pretend this never happened. Ryker and his posse won't scare me into backing down. I'm going to fight back.

***

Monica doesn't ask why I returned to the dorm at four in the morning. No cars passed me on the road, and I must have walked five miles in my ski boots until I reached campus. I wasn't even sure if my key card would work, or maybe they meant for me to stay out there all night, freezing to death, and they didn't expect me to come back.

Showering in hot water for thirty minutes doesn't completely thaw me out, but it helps. I lie in bed until the sun rises, but I don't sleep. My mind won't stop. I must pick up my phone a dozen times, about to call the police, my parents, or Chelsea or Brad, but in the end, I can't bring myself to do it. I want to handle this my own way, and if I call in help, it's like admitting defeat, saying I'm too weak to handle it myself. And there's also the shame and embarrassment I'm carrying around for trusting Ryker in the first place. I don't want to admit how stupid I was, that I fell right into the trap I was warned about.

Still, a tiny pathetic piece of me, somewhere in my chest region, hopes that the girls were lying about Ryker's involvement, and that they did this without his knowledge, but I don't know if they have it in them. And even if he didn't explicitly tell them what to do, they must assume he'd be okay with it.

When I see Winter and Aspen on campus the next day, they look surprised for just an instant, and then they ignore me. Petra watches me closely at practice the next few days, but she doesn't say anything. Ryker returns after only two days away, and he doesn't even look at me. I'm waiting to see if they'll try something else to push me into leaving, but it seems I've passed the test, and I'm allowed to stay, for now. My punishment has been dealt, and unless I commit another offense, I remain invisible.

A dark loneliness wraps around me, but with it comes anger and determination. Ingrid, Monica, Liam, and Misha are wary of me, I can see that. They don't want me to bring them down or get them involved in my "anarchy." So I stay quiet, trying not to stir anything up.

My new goal is to beat Petra Hoffman on the slopes. Before she left me on a mountain in the middle of the night, I never would have dreamed of beating her. She's Petra Hoffman, and it didn't seem within the realm of possibility. Now? Now it's what gets me up in the morning and gets me through the day.

The night before I'm scheduled to leave Stark for Christmas break, I find Ryker Black sitting on my bed in my dorm room, looking as if I should be happy to see him.

Ignoring him, I pull my suitcase out of the closet and begin to throw in some things from my dresser.

"Roxanne, will you look at me please? We need to talk. It's been nearly a month."

I'm tempted to walk right out of my room and leave him here, but I don't want to be a coward.

"I'm not here to apologize, if that's what you think," he begins.

"Then what are you here for, Ryker? You want me to leave Stark? Another test to see if I've got what it takes?"

"No. I think you've shown you've got what it takes. You're a fighter."

His admission gives me a twisted satisfaction.

"Then what are you doing here?"

He moves to the edge of the bed, and he'd better stay there. I don't want him getting too close.

You chose to stay. Does this mean you've accepted the way things are?" He's almost whispering and I feel like shouting in his face. "I was afraid you'd leave after that night, part of me wished you would, because you make me crazy, but every day I see you I'm relieved."

It's as close to an admission as I'm going to get that he, at the very least, was on board with what the girls did, and most likely, as they said, told them to do it. My heart sinks when I let go of that last thread of hope that maybe they'd been lying to me.

And knowing what he did, what he not only allowed, but probably directed, I can't believe he has the balls to say what he just did. Relieved to see me on campus? "Are you kidding me? No, I don't accept the way things are around here and unless they change, I never will."

What does this mean about our arrangement? You're going home for break. What about our promises to each other?"

And we're right back to where we were that very first encounter, him in my dorm room, and me thinking he's got to be delusional. I was lost in the woods in the middle of the night, in a snowstorm, and I'm lucky I got out of there without any permanent damage. All because of his little minions. And he thinks I still want to kiss him behind closed doors and continue being ignored the rest of the time? I'd kick him right in the balls if he was standing up. Any pity I had for his familial situation and social ineptness is entirely gone.

This is our new arrangement, Ryker. You will continue to ignore me as you always have. You won't speak to me again. And I'll sleep with whoever I damn well please here at Stark and home in Vermont. Now, get the hell out of my room."

Ryker looks murderous, and I'm shocked that I'm not afraid. He seriously looks like he wants to punch something. Or someone. But despite his admission that he thought he'd successfully scared me off after leaving me stranded in the woods, I'm not scared that he'll hurt me. He just stands up from my bed, fists clenched, chest heaving, and glares at me with such heat, I'm surprised there's no steam coming out his nostrils. And then he storms off, slamming the door behind him.

Ha. Ryker Black has some diva in him, that's for sure.

I allow a moment of humor at the situation, and then I sink to the floor, completely and utterly drained. That took all my bravado, but I pulled it off, and I'm damn proud of myself.

Chapter 19

The last thing I expected when I came home for Christmas was to be ready to return to Stark after the week was up. Being back in my hometown, seeing all the familiar faces, and especially sleeping in my own bed and having my parents dote on me, well, it was amazing, but I wasn't ready to go soft yet. I needed to hold on to my outrage through the end of the ski season. If I allowed myself to have too much fun at home, to get too comfortable, I wouldn't return to Stark. That was the truth. I couldn't enjoy it too much, or I'd never get back on the plane to Denver.

It was a whirlwind of skiing and Christmas parties, and no one seemed to notice that underneath it all, I was simmering with barely-contained fury over what had happened to me back at Stark.

When I return to my dorm room after a long day traveling, Monica is already there, lying on her bed with a laptop, listening to Justin Bieber. She blinks a few times when I walk in, apparently surprised to see me.

"You're back." Yup, she wasn't expecting me.

She shuts her computer and sits up.

"Classes and training start again tomorrow, so yeah, I'm back."

Monica wrings her hands nervously. "I really didn't think I'd be seeing you again, Roxie."

"Sorry to disappoint you." No wonder they'd all been acting so wary of me after my blow up at DH.

"It's not that, Roxie. You have no idea how happy I am that you're back. It's just, after you went after Ryker at DH in front of everyone, and then he dragged you outside, I guess we thought if he didn't do something right away, then he was just waiting for the semester to end so he could kill your scholarship for the rest of the year."

I sigh. At one point, I might have thought she was paranoid, but the thing is, she's right. He did do something right away, and assumed I'd probably leave on my own accord. But I didn't. Maybe I should have, but I don't want to give up.

Monica is watching me closely, probably wondering if I'm hiding anything from her. I want her to trust me, but I don't think I want her to know how stupid I was going off with Petra, Winter and Aspen, who had been nothing but hostile to me in the past. So, I shrug.

"Well, they told me to stay away and I listened this time. I'm done with Ryker and the posse, and it's over now."

Her body sags with relief. "That is really good to hear, Roxie. I heard from Olga over break, and she's mad at herself for what she did, for getting wrapped up in Ryker. I think she's still a little obsessed with him, so I didn't say anything about you, but I wouldn't want you to end up in her shoes -- getting kicked out, I mean."

"Are you going to keep treating me like a ticking time bomb or can we be real friends now?"

"We've always been real friends, haven't we?" Monica asks, though I can tell she knows what I'm talking about.

"It's not that I expect you to take a fall with me, Monica. I wouldn't want you to get in trouble because of my actions, but I guess it'd be nice to have a little bit of moral support, at least here in our room, behind closed doors, where we aren't being bugged."

She stands up then and puts out her arms for a hug, which I accept.

"I'm sorry," she says with sincerity when we pull away. "I was so afraid I was going to lose you too, right after losing Olga, that I just didn't know what to do. And, well, I was a little mad at you, but I get it. I even respect you for it."

"You were mad because I didn't listen to all your warnings, I get it." I might not like it, but I'm willing to forgive her, if it's even something that needs forgiving.

"So, tell me about your break back in Vermont. Are your friends going to come back to visit us? They're cool, Roxie. I'm jealous you've got them. Since I left for Stark in the eighth grade, I've pretty much lost touch with everyone from Michigan."

"Yeah, I know I'm lucky. What about the rink you skated at before coming here? Don't you go there still when you're home?"

"Yeah, but by now most of the girls I skated with have graduated or quit. I stopped practicing with girls my age when I was eight."

"So, have you seen Liam since you got back?" I knew they were still acting like a couple, but I really hadn't spoken with her about it since Thanksgiving.

She smiles. "Yeah, he was over in the room earlier. Misha went home with him for Christmas. Russia's too far for only a week. You know, I should thank you for making him dance with me that night. That was when it all started for us."

I hadn't thought she'd noticed that maneuver. "I didn't really do anything besides make it harder for him to avoid what he really wanted. Liam liked you before that, Monica, I could tell, he just isn't the kind of guy who goes after it. He wasn't sure what to do, with you two being friends and skating partners."

"Not like Ryker, who knows exactly what he wants, girls or otherwise, and just takes it."

My heart squeezes at her words. "Can we not mention him, like, ever again? Let's pretend all the stuff that went down last semester never happened, okay?"

Monica nods, understanding, and when we get together with Ingrid, Misha and Liam the next day, I have a similar discussion with them. I tell them they don't have to worry about me getting kicked out or getting them in trouble. It's over now, and I don't want to talk about it ever again. It's a relief when they don't pry, though I can tell by the way they glance at each other that all of them believe there's more to it. To be honest, I still wonder if I'm off the hook with the posse, or if it'll never really be over. I do know I'm done with Ryker; at least, I'm done with whatever it is we were doing together, or not doing.

Any worries I had about growing soft were for naught because as soon as I see Petra at the training hut the first practice back, I'm practically vibrating with the need to crush her. On the slopes, that is. She gives me a haughty look that might even be considered a sneer, and I just look away. I can play the ignoring game too.

Over the next couple of weeks, Rocco and Lia give every indication that my performance at practice is exactly what they were hoping for from me. Neither of them are the type of coach who gives much praise, but their lack of frustration directed at me, and their simple nods of approval, tell me everything I need to know. I'm ready to race.

With the exception of a few very talented individuals, most Stark athletes under age sixteen are still racing USSA, which means they will go to different races than the rest of us, who are racing FIS. All the seniors and juniors, and some sophomores, race FIS; apparently, if you're still at USSA level by that age, you aren't Stark caliber.

The FIS racers have three different competitions in January and early February. Depending on our rankings after that point, some of us will go to Europe for a couple of weeks in late February and early March to complete the season.

Our first FIS race is in early January in Aspen, and it's a four-day event, with two days of GS and two days of slalom. Even though these are tech races, and not my strongest, I do much better than I have in the past, and my FIS points are already lower than last year. My points qualify me for the first Nor-Ams race of the season at the end of January. It's called the Beaver Creek Carnival and it's one of the most competitive races in North America. It features only speed races, downhill and super-G, my favorites, and my best chances at beating Petra.

Petra might think she's being discreet, but I know she watches me. At practice, on campus, wherever I go. Ryker might have been right about one thing, after all. She feels threatened by me. And as my times at races close in on her, she might even have reason to be.

Beaver Creek is over three hours from Stark Springs, and we leave Monday morning, not to return to Stark again until the following Monday. The snowboarding teams are part of the Beaver Creek Carnival as well, and Stark has taken over one of the hotels at the base of the mountain. It's pretty unusual to host ski racing and snowboarding at one event, but it adds a festive layer to the atmosphere, and draws an even larger crowd.

Training on downhill and super-G gates is mostly impossible to do except for the days leading up to a race. For starters, the courses are very long, and it requires closing down too much terrain to the public. But even without that issue, the courses require netting (since lots of skiers crash or slide off the course at high speeds), and it's tricky to set up a challenging speed course. Not to mention the whole danger element. Women downhill racers regularly hit 50 MPH. So, we get three days of course inspection and training runs before the actual downhill race itself on Friday. Then we get one day off before the super-G race on Sunday.

The mountain village is already packed with athletes on Monday night when Ingrid and I search for somewhere to get food. As soon as we arrived late morning, we hit the trail. We weren't allowed to set up gates, which was actually a nice break, as far as I was concerned. I know I'm improving with all the gate training, but sometimes a girl just needs to go fast without any restrictions and for no other reason than the pure rush of speed on snow. After getting to do that all day, I'm happy and hungry. A rare combination, and it won't last long.

We slip into a burger joint and the place is hopping. I'm craving red meat at the moment, and we're able to snag two stools at the bar when a couple leaves. I'm not really paying attention to anything, just watching a Chet Preston film on one of the televisions above the bar, when I hear someone say my name.

"Roxie Slade? Whoa, hi."

I glance behind Ingrid and see a cute guy, dark hair peeking out from under a beanie. It takes a second before I recognize him. My first kiss. I'm not even sure what his name is. Something that starts with a "C"... I think.

"Hey!" I stand up, unsure whether a hug is appropriate, but hoping it will cover for me forgetting his name. "What are you doing here?"

"I'm racing tomorrow, you?"

"Yeah, me too. Who do you race for?"

"Canadian National Team. You're at Stark now, right? I hear you're tearing it up." Huh? He's heard about me?

"I don't know about that, but yeah, this is my first year at Stark." And quite possibly, my last. "Oh, this is my friend and teammate, Ingrid Koller." I gesture to Ingrid, who's spun around and is taking in the exchange.

"Carter Leduc. Nice to meet you, Ingrid."

"You too, Carter." And then Ingrid blushes. Blushes! This just keeps getting better and better. And by better, I mean worse.

Last time I saw Carter was two years ago at a post-race party at someone's house in Sugarville. He was in town for the race, leaving the next morning. I don't even remember who was throwing the party, but it was getting pretty rowdy. I was stone-cold sober myself, but I think that Carter was high because he smelled like pot when we kissed. He'd been into me all night, and he was cute, and I assumed I'd never see him again, so I let him kiss me in the laundry room. Yeah, I was sitting on a dryer when I felt a boy's tongue on mine for the first time. It was not romantic. Like, at all.

Carter orders a beer, and when the bartender turns away I ask quietly, "Are you twenty-one?"

"Just," he says with an eye-roll. "Drinking age in the U.S. is whack. It's worse than speed limits when it comes to no one paying attention to the law. You can smoke, vote, pay taxes, but you can't have a beer. Ridiculous." Right, so I was fifteen and he was nineteen when that all happened. Not totally sketchy, but bordering on it. "Wait," Carter asks. "When can you legally smoke pot in Colorado?"

"Twenty-one, I think," I tell him and he just shakes his head.

"A beer before racing, huh? Is that a Canadian thing?" Ingrid asks, and I resist the urge to smack my forehead. She can be so awkward sometimes.

Carter raises one eyebrow. "I have a beer every night. Been doing so since I was maybe fifteen. Don't worry, love, it's rarely more than one or two. And I almost never race drunk." He winks at Ingrid, picks up the beer that was placed on the counter, and takes a healthy sip, watching me over the rim of the glass.

I glance around behind him, trying to see who he came here with, and wondering if he's going to leave soon. I really just want to eat my burger and go to bed in the room I'm sharing with Ingrid. I don't feel like dancing around my awkward history with this guy.

Carter takes a step closer to me and begins to lean down to say something in my ear, but I'm not listening, because my eyes have locked on Ryker, who's sitting in a booth on the other side of the restaurant. He's watching me, and it's the first time I've caught him doing so since our run-in before Christmas. He's actively ignored me when we've crossed paths at the gym or anywhere else, but I've felt his eyes on me when I'm not looking. That's the thing about Ryker Black: even his stares are intense enough to be felt.

It takes a moment before I realize Carter is trying to give me his phone number. Before I can break the stare-down with Ryker, Carter sees where I'm looking.

"What's it like going to school with Ryker Black?" he asks.

I hesitate, unsure how to respond, but Ingrid beats me to it. "We don't talk about him," she says, totally serious. Oh, Ingrid.

But Carter just nods like he understands her completely. "Yeah, that's probably smart. You don't want to mess with that dude."

Just like every time I've heard Ryker's name recently, it feels like a little hand that's holding my heart region squeezes its fist, reminding me that he's still got power over me. On top of that, hearing Carter echo what Brad had overheard others say about Ryker is a little unnerving, but I refuse to contemplate what's behind it. Ryker's life is no longer my business, not that it ever was.

"So, Roxie," Carter continues, "we should hang out this week. I'm here until Monday. Let's get each other's numbers so we can meet up."

"I don't think I'll have time, Carter. This is an important race for me, and I'm going to be lying low."

And then Ingrid, of all people, pipes up telling him we've got tons of free time, and would love to meet up with him. "The Canadian Team's staying at the hotel across the street from us," she adds, letting him know exactly where he can find me.

Carter doesn't push to get my number, but I have a feeling we'll be running into him again. My eyes swing back to Ryker when Carter heads over to a table with five other guys, some wearing Canadian Team hats or jackets. Ryker's speaking with three people, and though I can't see their faces well, they look to be in their thirties or forties. He gets up then, and I watch as he walks over to Carter's table, and each guy at that table stops whatever they're doing to look at him.

It's that same reverent, fear-inspired look I've seen Stark students get when Ryker enters a room, and it's eerie seeing some of the best ski-racers in the world, most of whom have at least three or four years on Ryker, treat him with the same deference. My stomach drops while my heart rate picks up. Part of the reason I've kept fighting is that I assumed the whole King Ryker thing was confined to Stark; that, despite what I'd heard, no one outside our little bubble would treat him with that odd mixture of devotion, awe, and fear that follows him at Stark.

I'm clearly in way over my head, and the word *mafia* keeps swirling around, in and out, as if Ingrid is speaking it out loud, not in my memory. Everyone at the table turns to look at Carter, who's getting paler by the second. He nods, Ryker nods, and then Ryker looks at me, just for an instant, before returning to his table.

"What was that?" Ingrid murmurs beside me, but all I can do is shake my head. I haven't even spoken to Ryker in nearly two months, and he's still messing with my head.

Chapter 20

It takes more effort than I'm prepared to admit, but I manage to stop thinking about Ryker at about midnight, and instead visualize racing downhill at top speed until I fall asleep. When we wake eight hours later, a certain someone is still lingering on the periphery of my thoughts, threatening to overtake my concentration, but all it takes is the sight of Petra eating breakfast at the hotel to snap me back to my goal for this competition.

We get three training days before race day, and on the third day, our times on the course determine our starting numbers for the official race, with the lowest numbers going to those with the fastest times. Each morning after breakfast, Rocco and Lia take us for a course inspection, observing where the gates are placed, and where the slope dives and plateaus. The course is different each day, but not by much, and it's on the same trail. By the time we're done inspecting and training, we're exhausted. It's almost more intense than racing, because we can't actually fully release all the adrenaline building up until race day. I remember this from the downhill race in Maine, the growing anticipation, and the utter exhaustion each afternoon.

Fortunately, Ingrid is my hotel-mate, and she is totally down with going to bed at 8 PM each night, so I'm getting plenty of sleep. I also want to avoid seeing certain people, and it helps when we don't leave our hotel room except to practice and eat.

I do well on the training day that sets our bib number, but nothing spectacular. Petra does better. I'm accustomed to having a single digit on my bib, but just being in the top fifty amongst this crowd is a decent position to start with. I'm number 48, the second-ranked Stark female, and Petra is 21. She's aiming for a top-ten finish, which is a stretch, but would really show the world that she's an all-around threat in every discipline.

As I watch her ride up the lift ahead of me, I remember that she wanted me gone. *They* wanted me gone -- Ryker wanted me out of his life, and they were willing to push me to the edge to make it happen. They didn't just want to scare me, they were willing to harm me as well. And it wasn't even because of my skiing abilities, which I've proven are good enough; it was because I brought their little reign over the students into question.

But I'm still here, training, and racing, and getting closer to beating Petra Hoffman. Today might be the day. If I can beat her, prove that I'm good enough, then I can leave at the end of the school year with dignity.

It's a clear day, and the main lift takes us over the half pipe, where snowboarders are practicing. I've seen Ryker on the pipe at Stark countless times now, and as usual, my eyes find him; even wearing all his gear, I know how he moves. The riders have competition tomorrow, and they've got today off. For just one brief moment, the anger and embarrassment associated with him slip away, and they're replaced by affection and yearning. The fist squeezes, and I miss him. I shouldn't, I *really* shouldn't, but I wish things were different so badly. He was right though, I did want to be his girlfriend, I just got impatient and frustrated with the whole situation. And it's for the best he shut me down and reminded me who he is before I fell even harder. Because I did fall. And I hate that.

By the time we get to the top of the lift, I've recovered and can fake it even with myself, pretending that I never felt anything, that there's no longing burning inside me for something I cannot and will never have. Instead, I've brought the pain of rejection and humiliation to the surface, let the storm of fury inside me rage, pushing away the emotions I've now deemed as weak. Those feelings get me nowhere. Nowhere but stranded in the woods, that is.

I'm racing later in the queue than ever before with bib number 48 of about eighty athletes, as this race is even more competitive than the one in Maine last season. Racing early is almost always an advantage. For starters, the weather can change on a dime, and it often changes for the worse. But the real difference is that the course gets rutted out as more and more racers take the same line down the hill. Occasionally, if a racer rides the course just right, the ruts can be used to her advantage. If the racer skis her edge perfectly, the hard-packed snow, often ice by the end of the day, is actually faster than soft snow. But if the skier goes wrong at any point, drops a turn too soon or loses an edge, the ruts on the course and the icy terrain can make a little mistake a big one.

I'm an optimist though, and I think that I've got an advantage. The snow in Vermont is rarely soft and fluffy like the stuff in Colorado, and we usually get a lot less snow in general. I've noticed my Stark teammates complain about the snow on days that would be considered excellent conditions back in Vermont. In short, Colorado skiers are snow snobs, and therefore, they can't handle ice and hard terrain as well as I can. That's my logic. Sure, not everyone here trains in Colorado, but Vermont is notorious for its black ice, and if the course gets black today, I'll be in my element while others might be scared.

So as I jump up and down and swing my arms, trying to stay warm by the starting gate, I grin when I hear a coach telling her racer about black ice on the steepest part of the course.

Closing my eyes, I do one last visualization of the course, which we went through several times earlier this morning. After going out of the start, it's nearly flat for the first two gates before it takes a sharp plunge. It's crucial to hit that turn right in order to gain as much momentum as possible going through the first steep section. There's another brief plateau before the course hits a second wall, and that's where the black ice has formed. Without a perfect ski edge, slipping is unavoidable on black ice. Many racers do slide and lose time, and on a downhill course at the speed we're going, some racers fly completely off the course and injure themselves. Up here at the start, we usually don't hear about the crashes unless it causes a delay, and so far I haven't noticed any.

That's another reason being at the beginning of a race is the best. Once racers hear about a crash, it's hard to remain as aggressive. Even subconsciously, I think everyone backs off just a bit and becomes more tentative when a girl ahead of them gets hurt.

When they call my name and number, Lia removes the giant coat from over my shoulders and pats me on the shoulder. She never says anything right before I line up my skis. She lets me stay in my own head, not wanting to break my concentration. And right now, I'm thinking about how hard I'll push right out of the gate. My heart is already racing with anticipation. I don't know how Petra's run went, but I know that my muscles are in attack mode, and her spite has something to do with the fire burning as I kick back with all my might and rush forward.

Racing is a blur, as it always is. I'm wrapped up in executing each turn I've visualized beforehand, in the electric surge when I hit the turn just right, the momentum I feel picking up as my edge glides in just the right spot. I steel myself for the black ice as the course drops to a steep vertical, and even though I know it's there, can see the giant sheet of it as a blur ahead and then underneath me, I don't feel its slippery surface. That means I hit it perfectly; my instincts from years of skiing on ice took hold and I just got my edge right where it had to be.

I'm in perfect position for the next turn, hitting it high, and I can tell that the racers before me slid too low on this turn after slipping on the ice, because I haven't come anywhere near the ruts. This is the section that will make or break it, and my adrenaline surges with the speed I take through the bottom half of the course, having lost nothing to the black ice. There's a roar when I pass the finish line, and I can barely hear the announcer over the beating of my heart, but I know without a doubt, that was the best run of my life.

It takes a few minutes before my breathing slows and I recover from the disorienting effects of going full tilt. But when I do, my legs nearly give out. Not from fatigue, but because I'm in third place. *Third* place. Third place! No. Did I hear that right? Is that even possible? Once the first twenty or thirty racers do a run, the placings for the top ten finishers are usually set. I've raced forty-eighth, and I just shattered almost every single racer's time. Did the clock break?

When I go through the coaching and racers exit, which holds back cheering fans with a large net gating, my head is spinning. People I've never seen before are cheering, and my race is playing on repeat on a giant screen. It feels like I'm in a dream. Rocco approaches me and he's smiling as if he's the one who just had the best run of his life, and he wraps me in a hug, the first time I've ever seen him do that to anyone after a race.

"Did the clock break? Am I really in third?" I can't help but ask as I click out of my skis, which Rocco carries for me.

"You are, and unless someone else pulls off what you just did, you're going to be standing on the podium with two world cup gold medalists. You need to watch the playback, Roxie, it's remarkable."

"Yeah, okay, where?"

He guides me over to a tent, and I stiffen when I see that Petra is in there, watching a television and looking completely pissed off. The commentator is speaking about me. "Slade was several seconds off a podium time before she hit the black ice, and then, watch this, Paul," the woman says.

I watch myself in slow motion as my bottom ski digs into the black ice, and my top ski barely even hits the ground. From this angle, it almost looks like I'm lying down on the incline.

"She goes over that sheet of ice as if it's not even there. Instead of sliding down and losing momentum, she uses it to pick up speed."

"Incredible," the woman adds. I have to agree with her. I've got no idea how I pulled that off, especially as I watch clips of other skiers going over that same spot, and each one of them loses their edge. There's no avoiding it, it would seem. Except when I go. The ice wasn't black when the first few racers went, and the commentators remark on the unfairness of that, but I can't agree. It seems to me that the black ice worked in my favor.

A normal teammate, team captain, at that, would congratulate me. Even if it's not heartfelt and filled with jealousy, that's what anyone would do. But Petra Hoffman isn't normal, and she doesn't say a word to me when she leaves the tent.

My feet are glued in place as I continue to watch the screen in amazement. My name and time and place keep flashing on the bottom with the other top finishers, who of course I recognize as ski legends. I just can't process that this really happened. When Ingrid's form appears on the screen, the commentators talk about Stark Springs Academy, and that Petra Hoffman had a great race, sliding into a tenth place finish until I came along and bumped her into eleventh.

The difference between tenth and eleventh at a competition like this one is almost as tragic as the difference between third and fourth. She wasn't about to get on the podium, but the top ten is sort of a thing. It's the names that make the main scoreboards, and the people who make the most money, though I won't be taking any of the money I won today. Unless or until I know I'm not racing in college, I won't lose my NCAA eligibility. Just as my eighth place finish in Maine seemed like a fluke, my results today seem too good to be true.

The reality of the situation begins to sink in when I find my ski coat that one of the assistant coaches brought down from the top, and see that my phone is blowing up with messages. Right. My friends and family at home are watching this. Live. I've even got messages from random people I hardly keep up with who either trained with me at some point at triple-S or went to school with me.

Ingrid's scream snaps me back from reading my text messages. "You are a hero, Roxie!" She runs over to me, as best she can still wearing her ski boots, and lifts me in a hug. I've never seen her so enthusiastic. About anything. "And now I'm going to scold you. You just podiumed at the Beaver Creek Carnival and you're in this tent, all alone, reading text messages?"

"Well, what was I supposed to do? Hey, you rocked that run yourself, lady! You sure didn't race like someone who hates super-G."

"Well, we all heard about your race up at the start, and it got me all pumped up. All these racers who didn't think they had a shot at a top finish saw that you did it, and it's like the spirit of Roxie Slade seeped into us and we were hyper to race!"

Ingrid has lived in the United States since she started Stark nearly five years ago, but every once in a while, she says something that reminds me English is not her first language. Like the "spirit of Roxie Slade" or "hyper to race." Is she just weird or is it a language thing?

"Oh, and did I mention that you beat Petra?" Ingrid asks mischievously.

I grin back at her.

"You never said anything but I could see it. You've been after her since Thanksgiving. Whatever you were trying to prove, Roxie, I'm pretty sure you've accomplished it."

Have I? Well, shit. I've not only proven that I'm strong enough to stay at Stark, but I've beaten the girl who thought I didn't belong. It's exactly what I wanted. To make them, or *him*, sorry for what they did. He'll regret that he tried to make me leave, and when I do at the end of the year, when I don't come back, that's when I'll really be making a statement.

Chapter 21

"You like him, don't you?" I ask in disbelief. Ingrid Koller, straight-edge, rule-following Ingrid, is dragging me to a hotel party with the Canadian team.

"What? He's cute. But that's not why I think we should go. It's because you just placed third, and we can't just sit in our hotel room watching TV. We need to go out and celebrate. I've heard that lots of people will be there, so it's not like we're doing anything wrong."

My eyes narrow. "Like who?" If she thinks we're not breaking any rules, this is either a very clean, low-key gathering, or Ryker is already attending. Which doesn't necessarily mean we'll be welcome, actually.

"Sven and Player were talking about it on the elevator. They even asked if we were going."

My hands clench. Ingrid doesn't know what they did to me, but surely Sven and Player are aware of what went down that night. Do they want to be friends again, now that I've raced well? Do they think I would want that, allow it? As soon as this semester is over, I hope to never see them again. If they try playing another game, using me somehow, I'm not going to play into their hands.

Ingrid continues, "Besides, we don't race again until Sunday. You should probably sign some boobs, isn't that what famous American athletes do?"

"Has anyone ever told you how weird you can be, Ingrid?"

She ignores my question.

My heart rate picks up when we step off the elevator on the third floor and the noise level indicates that a party is going on. "Sven said room 302," Ingrid says before knocking on the door.

Someone opens it straight away, and judging by how we have to squeeze our way into the tightly-packed room, the person must have been pressed against the door.

I'm tempted to turn right around and leave, but Ingrid is determined to find Carter, who will hopefully get the hint that I'm not the one interested and give her some attention. Though I'm not so sure Ingrid would know how to handle that kind of attention. This seems like a bad idea in so many ways, yet here I am. I'm good at following through with bad ideas, it turns out.

When Ingrid finds him and taps his shoulder to say hello, he smiles for an instant, looks behind her at me, and freezes. I'd suspected this, and now it's been confirmed. "I'm going to find the bathroom," I tell Ingrid, turning quickly to leave before she can question me. Of course I don't need the bathroom. We just got here.

I wander through the crowded room and discover it's one of those suites that's got a common area and two bedrooms, and it's connected to another one just like it. The space isn't large, but there are so many bodies, and a few try to stop me to talk, that it takes me at least ten minutes to find him.

Ryker is sitting on a couch, Petra on one side, Aspen on the other. Sven and Player are sitting on a coffee table, facing them, but there are a handful of others around the group, trying to be a part of the circle. Typical. And of course he would be with the posse.

His eyes snap up as I approach and I almost growl, "We need to speak. Hallway." I tilt my head in that direction but he doesn't budge. "Fine, you want me to make a scene? I'm not afraid to do that, as you well know."

Ryker puts on a bored expression, but I trust nothing about him at this moment, not even his expression.

"Did you tell Carter Leduc to stay away from me?"

Ryker shrugs. "Yeah." And then he takes a sip of beer like it's no big deal.

"Why? You don't have that right."

"Yeah. I do. I don't want those Canadian guys messing with Stark girls. You had a race to focus on, and you rocked it, so you should be thanking me. And I should never have to explain myself to you, Roxanne."

I take a step forward and point a finger at him. "Stay out of my business, Ryker Black. You have no right to interfere with my life anymore. You lost that right when you had them," I gesture to the girls beside him, "leave me stranded in the middle of the night, and I still stayed. I passed your little test, so don't you dare..." I stop my rant when I see that Petra is turning pale as a ghost and Aspen looks ready to bolt. Ryker, on the other hand, is standing up.

"What did you just say? When did I ever leave you stranded in the middle of the night?" he asks so quietly, so darkly, that I take a step back, bumping into someone.

It's Sven, and he answers before I can. "She didn't say *you*, she said *them*." He nods to the couch. "The girls."

Player is standing up now too, and he's glaring at the girls. "What did you do?"

"Nothing," Aspen blurts. "We tried to make her feel better after that outburst at DH. We felt bad for her. She just got lost when we went night skiing, and we looked for her, but..." She keeps rambling and then Petra speaks over her.

"It was just a joke. A stupid joke. You would've approved it, Ryker, but you were on business, and we didn't get to talk to you about it. We didn't know it was going to storm that night. She had a headlamp and a cell phone."

My voice is eerily detached, nearly calm, when I say, "No service, and the headlamp died. You know, Petra, did you want me to die out there?" I can't look at Ryker. What if Petra is right? What if this is what he would've wanted? Didn't he say something to me about that night? My anger at Aspen and Petra for trying to justify what they did is dampened by confusion.

Ryker doesn't turn to glare at the girls as Sven and Player are doing. He remains facing me, and I can't lift my eyes from his chest, which is rising up and down slowly, tightly, as if he's trying really hard not to flip his lid. I can tell that without looking at his face, but then his fingers are holding my chin and he forces my head up, my eyes on his.

"I have no idea what you are talking about, Roxanne. Enlighten me."

I can hardly believe it when my eyes threaten to fill with tears. Where is that coming from? Is it relief? I have no idea.

"Not here," I whisper, suddenly all too aware of the scene we're making.

He takes my hand and leads me out of the room, the crowd parting for him in a way that would be comical if not for the rest of the situation. I've got two dual emotions going on right now, and they can't coexist. One is the walls closing, like I'm going to be crushed and destroyed. The other is like the walls lifting, or a weight being pulled, no *thrown*, off my chest, so it's like I could fly, or float away, with weightlessness. I'd attribute it to post-race high, the sensation of being so happy with my awesome results while nervous about the next race and what it means, but I think it has everything to do with the guy holding my hand.

He takes me into the hallway, around a corner, and into a stairwell before he stops and turns to face me. "You're going to tell me exactly what happened, Roxanne. Right now."

My first instinct is to resist. It's humiliating and I don't know what to think now that it seems Ryker had nothing to do with it.

"Don't boss me around and then maybe I will."

He doesn't look amused. He just closes his eyes as if praying for patience and then leans his head back against the wall for a minute.

I ask, "Why did you stay away for almost a month and then show up in my dorm room saying all those things? You said something about me choosing to stay, and proving I was strong, about not expecting me to still be here after that night. I can't remember, but I thought you knew what they did. They told me it was your idea. That you told them to do it."

"Roxanne." He's speaking to the ceiling, his head still back. "I don't know what they did, so how am I supposed to answer that?"

"Answer it how you would if you didn't know what they did." Despite what I heard in that hotel room, I don't want to be a pawn in a game again. What if this is just another elaborate scheme? What if they're trying to win me back because of how well I did today? It could all be a lie. Even if I trust the way he looked at me back there, I don't trust myself.

"Roxanne," he nearly growls. "You know what happened that night outside DH. We gave each other ultimatums. I said accept. You said change. I didn't change, and I waited to see what you would do. When you didn't leave Stark, I thought, I hoped, that meant you accepted me as I am. As we are."

I nod slowly. "And I thought you had punished me for challenging you. For calling you out at DH and then telling you I hated the Stark ways, your ways, I guess."

"I *didn't* punish you, Roxanne. That's the problem. Maybe I should have, but I couldn't. I didn't even consider it. It didn't cross my mind. Petra and Aspen have always been right about one thing. I don't treat you like the others at Stark."

At that admission, I tell him what happened when the girls took me snowmobiling, promising night skiing and apologies, and even though I didn't really believe them, I went anyway.

"Maybe I wanted to see how far they would go. I wanted to know the truth about them, about you."

We're several feet apart. I've moved to the staircase to sit down. It's the first time I've said out loud what happened, and it's exhausting.

"I got off the snowmobile I was sharing with Aspen, and they started driving away before I even reacted. I didn't have my skis. They got a little ways away and then told me that this was what you wanted. That you never really wanted me, you only wanted to use me as an example. I was too clingy, and it was time to teach me a lesson about challenging you, challenging the posse. And then they left."

Ryker walks quickly toward me as my chest starts to heave and I know I'm going to start sobbing. I try so hard to fight the tears, but they won't be pushed away and when Ryker squats in front of me, takes my hands, and tells me to let it out, there's no stopping it. Of course, that night on the mountain I held it together, but here on the stairway landing, with Ryker in front of me, I'm a mess.

He doesn't let me end the story there, though. He wants to know what happened after they left. It sounds so pitiful as I recount trudging around in that storm, trying to follow their tracks, crossing ravines, finally getting to a road only to have to walk five miles back to campus. All in my ski boots. I don't add that I was heartbroken, as I'm already pretty disgusted with how pathetic it all sounds.

Just the mere fact that Ryker is still here, listening to me sob and carry on, says a lot. But when I finally bring myself to look at him, and there's pain written all over his face, I fall, surrendering to that soaring feeling and escaping the crushing weight. He might be good at a lot of things, but he can't fake the look on his face, no matter what his acting skills are like. It's heartbreak, and it's for me.

"You believed what they said about me?" he asks when I'm done.

"Yeah, I guess. I mean, I hoped it was a lie. But you never came to talk to me or see me until the night before break, and then it sounded like you knew."

"How? What did I say?" Ryker's trying to remain gentle, but I can tell he's about to explode. He heaves slow breaths and his eyes go a little darker.

"I guess you were talking about our conversation outside DH, but it sounded to me like you were talking about something else. I don't even remember, Ryker, what it was, but it just made sense to me, in a way, that you were involved. You'd warned me. Monica and Ingrid had warned me. The girls who did it, Petra, Aspen, Winter, *they* even warned me before that night. It was like I had it coming all along."

"They'd warned you? About what?"

Now is probably not the time for more confessions so I remain vague, not mentioning Winter and Aspen's attack at the dorm. "Just to stay away from you and not to get in your way, or whatever."

Ryker moves from a squat to kneeling, so he's right in front of me on the stair. "Can I kiss you now, Roxanne?"

He's asked the question many times now, but it's the first time I shake my head. "No, Ryker."

"Why?" he asks it so softly, and I know that he already knew the answer.

"Because nothing has changed. I don't accept it and you won't change it."

"What if," he pauses, leaning even closer, "what if I do change things? What if you help me do it? Please, Roxanne. I want you with me. I don't want anyone else. Just you."

Lies.

Games.

The words are muffled, taunting, as Ryker continues to plead. "I can't stand being apart from you. I've wanted you, all of you, every defiant little part of you, since I first laid eyes on you at a race two years ago, Roxanne." His confessions silence the taunts. "It's not practical, it's not logical, and it's totally unreasonable, but it's undeniable. You've got me tied up and wrapped around your finger, and you don't even know it. Just tell me what you need, what you want, and I'll do it."

His dramatic declaration, coming when he's on his knees, no less, makes me suck in a startled breath. "You, this, everything, Ryker. It all seems too good to be true. It's like, I'm even thinking right now that this is part of a game. Like maybe you even somehow messed with the clocks at my race today. Because that felt too good to be true, too. Is there something I'm missing here? This doesn't make any sense. None of it makes any sense."

Oh, no, Roxie, do not cry again. Do. Not. Cry. I'm tempted to sprint up the stairs just to avoid showing so much weakness in front of him.

But then Ryker does the strangest thing. He laughs, and smiles so wide that I see the dimple. "You never say what I think you're going to say, Roxanne."

The grumpy sigh I let out is fake. His words make me smile, too. When we both start laughing so hard that we're clutching our stomachs, I think that he might have been right about us. *It's not practical, it's not logical, and it's totally unreasonable, but it's undeniable.* Whatever *it* is between us, he's got that right.

Epilogue

There's actually a woman at the bottom of the half pipe trying to get Ryker to sign her boobs. She's unzipped her jacket to reveal a tiny, overflowing, string bikini top. Ingrid is standing next to me, elbowing my ribs harder than necessary, and pointing. "See?" she says for the third time. "Boobs. What'd I tell you?"

Groaning, I don't bother pointing out that Ryker is a dude, a hot one, and that the half pipe tends to draw a different crowd than women's downhill skiing.

It's Sunday night, we're done competing, and it seems everyone has shown up to watch the final event at the Beaver Creek Carnival. Ryker has just finished his last practice run, and the crowd is roaring his name. He's ranked third, though judging by the volume of the hollers from female voices, he could be ranked last and it wouldn't matter much to them. Instead of going straight to the lift, Ryker takes the exit through the netting into the crowds, and the camera follows him as he makes his way past the woman thrusting her chest at him, and right in my direction.

He reaches me, and I'm too overwhelmed with his presence to be embarrassed about the fact that we're probably on live television. Ryker leans down and whispers in my ear, "I'm not playing any games with you right now, Roxanne. I just wanted to make sure you were here, watching, and you are."

"Ryker," I breathe out, trying to remain composed. "I told you I would be and I texted you five minutes ago. You could have just waved. We're on TV."

"I don't care. You haven't let me get rid of Petra and Aspen, so I wanted to make sure you were all right, too. Those girls are vengeful, as you well know."

I glance over my shoulder, where Ingrid and Sven stand as bodyguards. I'm not fooled by Sven's sudden appearance wherever I go without Ryker. And now that Ingrid's been let in on what happened that night, she's just looking for any reason to take down the culprits.

Ryker tugs me closer. "Just tell me what you want me to do about it. But it better be something. They aren't getting away with what they did."

After Friday night's revelations and declarations, Ryker said that the first step to show he wanted to change was that he would let me determine how to handle Petra, Aspen and Winter. It was a grand gesture for him, I knew this, but I'm not sure I want that power. I don't know what to do with it.

"I think we both know why you really walked all the way over here," I tell him, calling him out on his bullshit excuses. "You don't want me to be your dirty secret anymore, Black, do you?" I use the name he wouldn't let me call him that first day in the dorm, just to test him. Oh, and I know he hated it when I accused him of making me his "dirty secret" at DH that night. It really set him off. So yeah, I'm giving him a taste of his own medicine. Pushing him, seeing if he can handle it.

Ryker leans forward to put his lips to mine, but he doesn't kiss me like I expect. "You never were a secret, and certainly not a dirty one. I just never knew what to do with you, Ms. Slade."

And when he leaves me hanging, his lips only inches from mine, I ask him, "Are you going to kiss me now, or what?"

He smiles when he finally does, and my cheeks warm with the hoots and hollers that remind me this is anything but a private moment. I'm not entirely sure what Ryker Black is declaring to the world, or to me, right now, but I'm willing to find out. He's making a promise, that much I know, but it seems like the kind of promise a girl should brace herself for. Really though, is there any way to prepare for Ryker Black? It doesn't matter. I'm ready enough. He's already swept me up, and there's no denying it's going to be an epic ride.

Black Diamond is the first in the Stark Springs Academy Series.
Follow me on social media or join my email list to find out when
Double Black, the second book in the series, will be released!

Find me online at:

www.alideanfiction.com

www.facebook.com/alideanfiction

www.twitter.com/alideanfiction

www.goodreads.com/author/show/7237069.Ali_Dean

Want to be one of the first to read my books?

Sign up for the ARC list here: http://eepurl.com/bJ2G4T.

Want to hear about any sales, updates, or news I have?

Sign up for my mailing list here: http://eepurl.com/bJ-okv

Ali Dean is the author of the Pepper Jones series:

Pepped Up (Pepper Jones #1): http://amzn.to/1JZX7Mi

All Pepped Up (Pepper Jones #2): http://amzn.to/1UZlJpL

Pepped Up & Ready (Pepper Jones #3): http://amzn.to/1UZlJpL

Pep Talks (Pepper Jones #4): http://amzn.to/1Ph79EI

Pepped Up Forever (Pepper Jones #5): http://amzn.to/1VR7nW2

The Pepper Jones Collection (first three books in the series):
http://amzn.to/1L2GGVA

Acknowledgements

Editor: Leanne Rabesa

http://editingjuggernaut.wordpress.com/

Cover: Gotcha Covered Design

https://www.facebook.com/gotchacovereddesign/

A special thanks to Lindsay Brush Getz for her insight into the world of alpine ski racing. Also, a huge thank you to my publicist and beta reader, Ashley Blevins!

And to my readers... thank you so much for your enthusiasm! You are awesome.

Made in the USA
Middletown, DE
10 September 2016